"What Happened Back There... It Just Happened,"

Roxy told him. "It didn't mean anything. It was just the result of a weird situation. There's no reason to read anything into it. So let's just forget about it. Okay?"

But Spencer refused to let it go that easily. There was no way he was going to brush it off as meaningless.

"Okay?" she repeated when he didn't reply.

"Okay," he agreed reluctantly. "For now."

Roxy opened her mouth to say something more, but Spencer covered it lightly with his fingers. He leaned toward her, touching his mouth to hers, this time with a gentleness completely at odds with the reckless passion that had overtaken him before. Her eyes fluttered closed for a moment, opening only when he pulled away.

"For now," he repeated softly. "But this isn't the end of it, Roxy. Not by a long shot."

Dear Reader,

Happy Valentine's Day! This season of love is so exciting for us here at Silhouette Desire that we decided to create a special cover treatment for each of this month's love stories—just to show how much this very romantic holiday means to us.

And what a fabulous group of books we have for you! Let's start with Joan Elliott Pickart's MAN OF THE MONTH, *Texas Moon*. It's romantic and wonderful—and has a terrific hero!

The romance continues with Cindy Gerard's sensuous *A Bride for Abel Greene,* the next in her NORTHERN LIGHTS BRIDES series, and also with Elizabeth Bevarly's *Roxy and the Rich Man,* which launches her new miniseries about siblings who were separated at birth, THE FAMILY McCORMICK.

Christine Pacheco is up next with *Lovers Only,* an emotional and compelling reunion story. And Metsy Hingle's dramatic writing style shines through in her latest, *Lovechild*.

It's always a special moment when a writer reaches her 25the book milestone—and that's just what Rita Rainville has done in the humorous and delightful Western, *City Girls Need Not Apply*.

Silhouette Desire—where you will always find the very best love stories! Enjoy them all....

Lucia Macro

Senior Editor

Please address questions and book requests to:
Silhouette Reader Service
U.S.: 3010 Walden Ave., P.O. Box 1325, Buffalo, NY 14269
Canadian: P.O. Box 609, Fort Erie, Ont. L2A 5X3

ELIZABETH BEVARLY
ROXY AND THE RICH MAN

SILHOUETTE *Desire*
Published by Silhouette Books
America's Publisher of Contemporary Romance

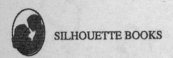

SILHOUETTE BOOKS

ISBN 0-373-76053-1

ROXY AND THE RICH MAN

Printed in U.S.A.

ELIZABETH BEVARLY

is an honors graduate of the University of Louisville and achieved her dream of writing full-time before she even turned thirty! At heart she is also an avid voyager who once helped navigate a friend's thirty-five-foot sailboat across the Bermuda Triangle. "I really love to travel," says this self-avowed beach bum. "To me, it's the best education a person can give to herself." Her dream is to one day have her own sailboat, a beautifully renovated older model forty-two footer, and to enjoy the freedom and tranquillity seafaring can bring. Elizabeth likes to think she has a lot in common with the characters she creates, people who know love and life go hand in hand. And she's getting some firsthand experience with maternity as well—she and her husband recently welcomed their firstborn baby, a son.

For Carol Conaway.

Thanks for helping me find the right road.

Prologue

There it was again. The dream.

Spencer Melbourne sat up in bed and stared into the darkness, shivering in the cool October breeze that rattled the blinds on his bedroom window. In spite of the chilly night air, sweat rolled down between his shoulder blades and streaked his bare chest. The damp white sheet lay at the foot of his bed in a tangle, leaving his naked body exposed to the autumn night. He raised a shaky hand to shove a fistful of damp black hair off his forehead and inhaled a deep, ragged breath, trying to steady his accelerated heart rate.

For as long as he could remember, he'd been having the dream. Usually once or twice a year, occasionally once or twice a month. But lately, it had been coming once or twice a week. And lately, it had grown far more vivid than it had ever been before. Every time the dream unrolled in his head these days, there seemed to be a little more to it, something new that hadn't been there before.

He dropped his head into his hands and tried to pinpoint exactly what had been different this time. Immediately, he recalled the face. Unlike before, this time he'd almost seen a face in his dream. A hazy oval shape of milky white, topped by a crop of short hair as dark as his own. But nothing more than that. No vivid blue eyes like his, no stark cheekbones or narrow nose or full lower lip like the features he saw every time he looked at his own image in the mirror. Nothing but a blur. That's all the face in his dream was.

Nevertheless, he knew who the face belonged to, and he knew the man was out there somewhere. Spencer had been certain of it in the deepest, darkest part of his soul since he was a child. And more than anything in the world, he intended to find the owner of that face. He didn't know how or when, but somehow, some way, he was going to find him.

Somehow, some way, Spencer Melbourne was going to find his brother.

One

Roxy Matheny was in the middle of cleaning out her newly inherited office when she acquired her very first client. But instead of giving her a thrill of exhilaration, the rapid knock on her outer office door only made her grumble in irritation. She was dressed in a pair of snug black bicycle shorts and a dirt-smudged, oversize T-shirt that read Eat It Raw At Ollie's Oysters. Her hair, the color of strong coffee, was half in and half out of a stubby ponytail. She was more than a little damp—and fragrant—from perspiration.

Not exactly the professional image she had hoped to project to any prospective client, she thought as she stared at the seemingly human outline silhouetted in the frosted glass of her outer office door. Still, a paying customer was a paying customer, right?

She glanced around the inner office, the tiny, confined area looking even less professional than she was at the moment. She was still hip-deep in her grandfather's old files, even after having tossed most of them into a half-crushed cardboard box. The sunlight struggling to shine through the window behind her was dulled by a good two decades of grime, and the ancient rolltop desk in the corner, not to mention the filing cabinets flanking it, were covered by an equally heavy layer of dust. Her phone wasn't connected yet. She hadn't hired a secretary. Nor could she afford one. She hadn't even had a chance to change the flaking gold lettering on the outer door from Bingo Matheny, P.I. to Roxanne Matheny Investigations, Inc.

She thought about ignoring whoever had come calling. She wasn't actually in business yet, and still had a bazillion things left to do before she could hang out her shingle. Then she remembered that she only had seventy-eight dollars and thirty-six cents in her bank account. She could use the cash this person would provide as a retainer up front. A girl had to eat, after all.

Wiping the sweat from her face with the hem of her T-shirt, Roxy strode to the outer office and wrestled with the rusty bolt on the door before finally yanking it free. A man stood on the other side, a rather unremarkable development that normally wouldn't cause her to look twice.

But look twice she did at this man, because he was dressed in a sleekly cut charcoal suit and crisp, white dress shirt, a too-too conservative, sapphire-colored necktie knotted expertly at his throat. By the way his black hair was cut and styled, Roxy was pretty sure he hadn't mistaken her office for Bonita's World of Unisex Hair downstairs. In fact, she couldn't imagine a single reason for this guy to be anywhere in her zip code. He just screamed dollar signs right down to the wing tips of his pointy-toed black shoes.

"Are you Bingo?" he asked.

The question threw her, not just because she had been so caught up in marveling at how he had made it this far without being mugged, but because his voice was as rich and refined as the rest of him. "Do I *look* like a Bingo?" she asked.

He seemed stumped by her reply. "I don't know. What does a Bingo look like?"

Roxy thrust a thumb over her shoulder, toward the photograph of her grandfather that still hung in the outer office. It had been taken in 1942, when Bingo was forty, and pictured her grandfather wearing a bowler hat tipped forward on his head and clutching a .45 at his waist. As always, he was frowning.

"That," Roxy told the man. "That's Bingo. My grandfather."

The man studied the photograph, glanced back at Roxy, then looked at the likeness of her grandfather again. "He doesn't look like a Bingo to me, either."

"Yeah, well, that's him. Bingo Matheny, last of the big-time gumshoes."

"Is he here?"

Roxy shook her head. "Nope. He's pushing up daisies at Rest-Ye-Well Fields in Baltimore."

"Oh." The man looked disappointed.

"Can I help you?"

"Are you a private investigator?"

She nodded, wiped her hand on her shorts and thrust it forward. "Roxanne Matheny, P.I."

The man stared at her outstretched hand for a moment before clasping it in his own. When he did, he gripped her fingers with confidence, pumping her hand three times before releasing it again. All in all, Roxy thought, it was a good, sturdy handshake, and his hand was warm and dry. She smiled. There was nothing like a guy with clammy hands to wreck an otherwise promising day.

"Come on in," she told him, stepping aside to allow him entry. "Excuse the mess. I'm just now moving into Bingo's office. He left it to me in his will."

"What happened to him?" The man entered somewhat gingerly, and walked by Roxy to pause in the middle of the outer office. "Did he die in the line of duty?"

She chuckled. "Um, I guess you could say that. Some guy caught Bingo in bed with his wife. The guy's wife," she clarified. "Bingo was never married. Not even to my grandmother."

The man's eyes widened in horror. "Someone murdered your grandfather in a fit of jealous rage?"

Roxy laughed again. "No, Bingo had a heart attack. Hey, he was ninety-five years old, after all. Even Bingo's old ticker couldn't handle the excitement of making love *and* getting caught in the act."

The man frowned. "You seem pretty cavalier about losing him."

She rubbed her forearm over her forehead, pushing her hair out of her eyes, then smiled sadly. "Don't get me wrong. I miss Bingo a lot. He was…well, pretty indescribable. But he lived a *very* full and long life. And he went exactly the way he wanted to go. It was a good time for him to move on to other things."

"Other things," the man repeated.

Roxy nodded. "So, how can I help you?"

Spencer Melbourne studied the woman before him and wondered if he might not be better off hightailing it to another agency. The only reason he'd tried this one was because he knew Bingo Matheny had done some investigative work for his father some years ago—a delicate matter the elder Melbourne hadn't wanted made public, and Bingo Matheny had kept a remarkably low profile and had seemed a person of integrity. Then, when Spencer had gone to look up Matheny's ad in the Yellow Pages, it had said missing persons was the company's specialty. Spencer needed to find his brother. A private investigator like Bingo Matheny had resources he didn't have himself.

Unable to help himself, Spencer took in Roxanne Matheny's attire and her sadly deteriorating office space. Of course, he reminded himself, it would make sense to hire a *good* private investigator. One who had some vague idea what he—or she—was doing.

"Um," he began, wondering exactly how to go about this without insulting her. It occurred to him then that she seemed awfully young. Perhaps considerably younger than his own thirty-four. "Just how long have you been in business?"

Her eyes widened just a fraction, and for the first time, Spencer noted how dark they were—nearly as dark brown as her hair.

"In business?" she asked. "Me?"

"Yes. How long have you been working in the investigative field?"

"Ummm," she said, stringing the syllable out over several time zones. Until then, her gaze had met his unfailingly. But now it ricocheted around the room like a drunken fly.

"Ms. Matheny?" he added when she seemed to have forgotten the question.

Her gaze met his again, then dropped down to her hands. She rubbed furiously at a streak of dirt on her palm as she replied. "Actually, I haven't been in business very long. But everything I learned, I learned from Bingo. I assisted him on a number of cases before becoming an investigator myself, all kinds of stuff."

She straightened and met his gaze pointedly again. "I'm fully licensed by the state of Virginia to practice as a private investigator. I grew up right here in the Washington, D.C., area, and I have better instincts than a bloodhound. Whatever you need done, I can do it. Divorce, corruption, extortion, missing persons..."

Spencer latched on to her last words. "Missing persons," he echoed.

"Aw, jeez, that's a piece of cake," she assured him with a snap of her fingers. Before he could counter otherwise, she rushed on, "Just let me get a little bit of information. Follow me."

Spencer did as she requested, wondering if he was making a big mistake in doing so. The inner office looked even worse than the outer office, carpeted in scattered paper and looking as if it hadn't had a good cleaning since the Bay of Pigs.

In spite of that, Roxanne Matheny, P.I., riffled through some documents on the desk until she located a pencil and a pad of paper, looked around for a chair, located an old wooden one with wheels and shoved a huge pile of file folders off of it and onto the floor. Then she settled her sneaker-clad foot on it and pushed hard, sending it wheeling across the room with an almost musical *squeakity-squeakity-squeak* until it came to a halt, perfectly positioned for seating, immediately in front of Spencer.

And he couldn't help thinking then that maybe Roxanne Matheny knew what she was doing, after all. He took a seat in the chair as she perched on the edge of the huge rolltop desk behind her.

"So you're looking for someone, huh?" she asked.

He nodded. "My brother."

She nodded back and scratched her pencil across the notepad. "When was the last time you saw him?"

Spencer bit his lip. This was where it was going to become a little difficult to explain. "I, uh, I haven't actually seen him."

The investigator's head snapped up, and she studied him through narrowed eyes.

"At least, I don't *remember* ever seeing him," he clarified.

"You want to elaborate on that for me?"

"I was adopted," Spencer told her. "According to my parents—my adoptive parents—when I was eighteen months old."

Roxanne Matheny scrawled something else on her notepad and said, "Gotcha. And you want to find out if you have any birth siblings, is that it?"

He shook his head. "No, I *know* I have a brother. A *twin* brother."

She eyed him levelly again. "How do you know that? Did your parents tell you that?"

"No, they never indicated any knowledge that I had any other siblings," he said. "I just know for a fact that I do."

"Look, Mr...." She arrowed her dark eyebrows down, as if she'd just now realized something. "What's your name, anyway?"

"Melbourne," he told her. "Spencer Melbourne."

"Look, Mr. Melbourne, I can use a couple of bucks as much as the next guy, but let me save you some money here. If you're just working on a hunch—"

"It's no hunch," he assured her.

"But—"

He knew he was probably going to regret telling her about it, but he heard himself say, anyway, "I have this dream."

She grinned at him, and for the first time, Spencer realized that she actually wasn't a bad-looking woman, in spite of her bedraggled appearance. When she smiled like that, she was almost…kind of…attractive.

"Hey, guy," she said, "we all have a dream. Mine is to win ten mil from Ed McMahon, buy a big ketch and head south for—"

"Ms. Matheny, do you mind?" he interrupted her.

Her smile fell. "Oh. Oh, yeah. Sorry." She poised her pencil over the notepad once again. "So you have this dream," she encouraged him.

Almost unconsciously, Spencer swiped his palms over his trousers, feeling anxious just thinking about it. "Yes. I've been having it since I was a child. There's not much to it, just that I'm with someone, someplace I don't recognize, and the other person…" How did he describe this without sounding like a stark-raving lunatic? "The other person looks just like me."

"So you've seen the other person's face?"

"No."

"Then how do you know he looks just like you?"

"I…I just…do."

He watched as she wrote some more, wondering if she was actually taking notes about his situation or writing something to throw out the window like, *I'm trapped on the third floor with a psychopath—call 911.* "Ms. Matheny?" he asked halfheartedly.

She held up her right hand, index finger extended, as she continued to write with her left. "Hang on," she mumbled.

She was probably trying to remember how to spell *psychopath*, Spencer thought. He opened his mouth to remind her that there was a *p* in front of the *s* when she looked up at him again.

"Okay, so you have a feeling you've got a twin brother out there somewhere."

"No, I *know* I have a twin brother out there somewhere. Have you ever done any reading on twins, Ms. Matheny?"

She shook her head. "No, I can't say that I have."

"It's fascinating. Of particular interest are the studies done on twins separated at birth and reunited later in life. There are a number of similarities between them, often things that would appear to be environmentally inspired, but which might possibly be genetic. There have been incidents of reunited twins married to wives who resemble each other, or who wear the same number of rings on precisely the same fingers, or who give their children the same names. It's not unusual for them to show up for their initial meetings dressed almost identically.

"And it's not unusual for twins to share emotional responses," he added quickly when she seemed about to interrupt him, "or feel a psychic connection to each other. Whether they know of each other's existence or not."

"And you've experienced this, um, this psychic connection...yourself, have you?"

Spencer closed his eyes and tried not to wince out loud. He knew he must seem crazy. He knew he must sound like one of those pathetic, dismal people who showed up in those awful infomercials touting paranormal hot lines. He knew Ms. Matheny was probably labeling him with any number of adjectives normally reserved for people who claim less than half a brain.

In spite of that, he opened his eyes, met her gaze evenly and told her, "Yes. I have experienced it myself."

"In what way?"

He'd been afraid she was going to ask that. Feeling suddenly restless, he rose and began to pace the tiny, stuffy room. "I just have these feelings sometimes, that come to me seemingly out of nowhere."

"What kind of feelings?"

When Spencer stopped pacing, he realized he stood only inches away from Ms. Matheny. Instead of returning to his chair, he sat beside her on the huge, sturdy desk and looked at her. Her dark bangs were threaded here and there with silver, and her brown eyes bore faint lines of laughter. Her mouth, too, though soft looking and full-lipped, was bracketed by faint lines. She wasn't as young as he'd initially thought, he realized. She was probably about his age. For some reason, the realization comforted him.

"A feeling that I'm not alone," he finally told her, his voice quieter than he'd intended it to be. "A feeling that there's another life out there that I'm a part of. That someone else is thinking about me. That...that I have a brother," he told her. "I just can't shake the certainty that I have a twin brother out there somewhere. And I'd like to find him, Ms. Matheny. Can you help me?"

Roxy nibbled the hard eraser on the end of her pencil and met her prospective client's blue-eyed gaze. Black hair and blue eyes, she thought wistfully. It was a combination of masculine features that had brought her trouble on more than one occasion. Still, there was little chance of anything happening between her and Mr. Melbourne. He was obviously nothing more than some rich eccentric, completely full of hooey. The two of them had absolutely nothing in common.

And there was no way on God's green earth that he was going to find who he was looking for, Roxy thought further, because who he was looking for just didn't exist on God's green earth. But he seemed so earnest, so troubled, so anxious to know the truth, that she couldn't quite force herself to tell him to forget about it.

"Are your adoptive parents still alive?" she asked him.

He seemed surprised by the question, but shook his head slowly. "No. They were well into their forties when they adopted me. They died within months of each other a little over a year ago. Why?"

Instead of answering, Roxy asked another question. "You got any brothers or sisters? In your adopted family, I mean."

Another shake of his head. "No. Why?"

"Any cousins, aunts, uncles, whatever?"

"A few. None to whom I'm close, though. Why?"

This time Roxy chewed her lip thoughtfully. "Don't take this the wrong way, but...you think maybe it's possible you're having these feelings so strong now because you've lost your folks?''

His blue eyes became icy as he retorted, "Are you suggesting I'm delusional?"

Roxy arched her brows philosophically. "Nope. Just maybe that you're lonely. Feeling a little unfulfilled."

She hadn't intended to insult him—heck, ninety percent of the population was lonely and unfulfilled, she thought, herself included. It was just a fact of life, not anything to be ashamed of. But Mr. Melbourne apparently didn't put much stock in her assessment of his life-style.

"Ms. Matheny, I'll have you know that I'm one of Washington, D.C.'s most prominent citizens."

Riiiight, Roxy thought. *That's why you're knocking on* my *door.* The guy might have money, as evidenced by his clothes. Okay, and good taste, too, she conceded for the same reason. But prominence? She doubted it. He was just some wealthy, lonely guy who had nothing better to do on a Friday afternoon than go slumming in her neck of the woods to see what he might find under an upturned rock. Oh, well. She supposed there was no harm in him believing he was important in the scheme of things, as long as it made him happy.

"Wow," she finally replied, hoping she sounded suitably impressed. "One of our most prominent citizens? No foolin'?"

"No fooling," he assured her, his voice sounding as it might if he had just bitten into something that tasted really awful. "I head up one of the largest communications corporations in the country. I have more investments and holdings than you can imagine. I'm a subscriber to the Kennedy Center, a member of the Smithsonian, a contributor to every fund that's worth anything, and I have the ear of any politician I want. And my family has been listed in the *Social Register* since the turn of the century."

"I'm a member of the Smithsonian, too," Roxy volunteered with a smile when he concluded his self-estimation. "Don't you love that ten-percent discount you get at the gift shops?"

"I'm not joking, Ms. Matheny," he told her. "I can afford any private investigator in this country."

"Yet you chose me," she said. "I'm flattered. Truly I am."

"I didn't choose *you*," he felt it necessary to clarify. "I really wanted to enlist the aid of your grandfather. I came here because Bingo Matheny did some work for my father a few years back and was decent enough to keep it under his hat."

"What kind of work?"

He hesitated. "I'd rather not discuss the particulars."

"Ooooooh," she said with a knowing nod. "Gotcha. Well, for what it's worth—and not many people know this—Prudence is my middle name."

He ignored her commentary and asked instead, "Look, do you want the work or not? Will you take my case?"

Roxy had never prided herself on her integrity, nor had she ever much had a soft spot in her heart for anyone or anything. But Spencer Melbourne got to her for some reason. The guy was just too puzzling for her to be able to figure him out.

Delusional as he was, he was still determined to find this brother who didn't exist. He could afford to spend a lot of money on a private investigator, and he would no doubt do so in his relentless—and, in her opinion, fruitless—search. So why shouldn't *she* be the one cashing the checks, instead of one of her more expensive, and infinitely less deserving, colleagues? Hey, as long as he had his checkbook on him, she thought, Roxanne Matheny was his man for the job.

"Okay, I'll take your case," she said, extending her hand toward him once again. "Now then. Let's talk about my fee. And I'm going to require a retainer up front..."

Two

The Potomac at dawn in late October was a beautiful thing, Roxy decided as she sat on the banks of the river with her knees drawn up before her. She gazed out over the water that rippled like wind-tossed silk, its dark surface catching the sunlight and dancing with it before throwing it back in diamonds. To her left downriver, coming toward her as they skimmed smoothly along the water's surface, were two long vessels, each propelled forward by a team of rowers. Breaking the silence of the morning were faint, but almost identical, cries rising from each of the teams. Staggered, but nevertheless harmonious, the team captains called out, "Stroke... stroke...stroke...stroke...stroke..."

A cool breeze redolent of autumn leaves nudged her hair into her eyes, and she absently pushed the stray tresses back behind one ear. The ground beneath her fanny was cold and still damp with dew, but Roxy didn't care. There was something so peaceful about the moment, so utterly still and wonderful, that she didn't dare move to disturb it. Serenity had been an infrequent companion in her life, and she wasn't such a fool that she would dare interrupt what little came her way.

The two sculling vessels and their teams passed her eloquently, their elegant profiles dark against the pink sky behind them, all the more graceful because of their simplicity. Although too far off for her to see him, she knew Spencer Melbourne manned a pair of oars in one of those craft, and that he would be pulling into a Georgetown boathouse a quarter mile on down in a matter of minutes. She knew because he had told her to meet him there at seven o'clock, and it was now twenty minutes before the hour.

Roxy stood and brushed off the seat of her black leggings before tugging her hooded, faded red sweatshirt down over her fanny, then shoved her hands into the pocket that spanned the front of the garment. So this was what rich people did to unwind, she thought as she picked her way carelessly along the riverbank toward the boathouse. Not a bad racket at that. But it would be a real bummer to have to get up this early every day. That was the best thing about being in business for herself. She could set her own hours.

Well, usually, she amended as she approached the door to the boathouse she had been told was owned by the corporation Melbourne headed up. Every now and then, she supposed she was going to have an early riser like him for a client, someone who expected to be doing business while most people were still quaffing their morning o.j. and trying to find their other shoe.

Roxy stifled a yawn as she turned the doorknob and entered the boathouse. She was going to have to give up her late nights in front of the TV as long as she was working for Spencer Melbourne. But that was just as well, she conceded. The reception on the feeble black-and-white was lousy, anyway, and nobody showed the old screwball comedies on the late show anymore. She always seemed to fall asleep to the sound of Arnold Schwarzenegger or Sylvester Stallone blowing somebody away. Not exactly the kind of thing a woman liked to snuggle up to at night.

Boathouse was a deceptive term, she realized quickly. This place looked more like a country club, complete with dark paneled walls, richly carpeted hardwood floors and scrollwork on the ceiling. As Roxy closed the door behind her, a woman twice her age and dressed almost identically as she was herself, entered through another door on the opposite side of the room, wiping her face with a towel as she approached.

"Can I help you?" the woman asked.

Roxy nodded. "Yeah, I'm supposed to meet Spencer Melbourne here at seven."

The woman nodded back. "I'll go get him."

She disappeared back through the door, and Roxy heard her call out, "Spencer! You're wanted out front!"

The woman strode back into the entry foyer again with her hand outstretched. "I'm Diana Brent. I'm vice president in charge of public relations for Melbourne Communications Systems."

Roxy took the other woman's hand and shook it. "Roxanne Matheny," she said without elaborating.

Diana Brent eyed her curiously, but didn't press the matter. Instead, she dropped Roxy's hand, looped her towel around her neck and said, "Spencer should just be a minute."

"Thanks."

With a final smile, Ms. Brent walked past her and ascended the stairs behind Roxy two at a time. The moment she disappeared from sight, Spencer Melbourne strode through the door opposite, and at the sight of him Roxy's mouth dropped open in astonishment.

He barely resembled the man she had met on their initial encounter four days before. Instead of the dark, perfectly put-together suit, he was dressed in well-worn, navy blue sweatpants and a gray sweatshirt, its front dark with perspiration and decorated with three huge letters—GWU. He, too, had a towel hanging around his neck, but his hair was still damp with sweat and falling forward over eyes that seemed even bluer today than they had on Friday. The moisture caused his hair to be curly in spots, and for some reason, Roxy's fingers itched to reach out and smooth the unruly tresses back in place.

Down, girl, she instructed herself. *Just 'cause a guy looks good in sweats, it doesn't necessarily make him sweatshirt material.*

"Ms. Matheny," he said as he approached her. Even his voice was more relaxed this morning than it had been Friday. "I'm sorry to get you out so early in the morning, but this really is the only time I'm going to have today to meet with you."

"No problem," she assured him. "What did you need to talk to me about?"

He glanced discreetly over his shoulder, then tipped his head toward the door through which he had entered. "Follow me," he said as he turned, his tone of voice indicating he had no doubt whatever that she would react as he bid without question.

"Jawohl," she muttered under her breath as she did just that.

She followed him through the door and into a room that appeared to be a sitting room of some kind, equipped as it was with a dozen couplings of leather-bound chairs situated for conversation. Like the foyer, it was paneled with some dark wood and splashed with color thanks to a massive oriental rug that spanned the floor in swirls of ruby, emerald, sapphire and gold. Outside the floor-to-ceiling windows, the Potomac flowed silently by, and at the center of the room was a huge crystal chandelier gleaming with soft yellow light. Beyond that room, Roxy followed Melbourne through another very much like it on a smaller scale, before coming to a kitchen.

"Coffee?" he asked as he paused by a sophisticated—and expensive-looking—maker.

"Yeah, please," she told him. "Black," she added before he could ask.

He filled two mugs emblazoned with the Melbourne Communications Systems logo, handed one to Roxy, then proceeded once more without a word. Again, she followed him obediently, until he paused before a door at the back of the building and extended his arm to indicate she should precede him through it. When she did, she found herself in a very small room decorated in much the same style as the others had been. But where the others had been very formal and had seemed more than a little stuffy, this room was cozy and inviting.

Painted a deep forest green, two walls consumed by shelves housing books on fly-fishing, boating and business, the furnishings old and elegant, the tiny space was obviously intended for Melbourne's use alone. This was his private retreat in a house where many people came and went, a place where he could come or go when he needed to concentrate or meditate. Roxy wasn't sure how she could be so certain of this when she knew so little about the man. But somehow, she knew this was *his* room.

When he closed the door behind them and moved silently to the window to gaze out at the river, she was even more certain of her assumption. He exuded a sense of belonging here, of being comfortable, and relayed his possession of the room without ever saying a word. Roxy glanced around again and noted a few personal touches—two small trophies perched atop one of the shelves, photographs hanging on the wall that featured Spencer Melbourne in various stages of athletic attire surrounded by similar-looking men and a battered rugby ball tossed carelessly on the couch.

It was a guy room, plain and simple. And for some reason, the recognition of that made Roxy smile.

When he still offered no indication that he intended to speak, she shifted her weight a little restlessly from one foot to the other. He must have heard the small rustle of sound her action generated, because he suddenly spun around and stared at her. For a moment, he looked as if he had forgotten she was there. He also looked as if he were completely lost and had no idea where to turn.

"Um," Roxy began. She cleared her throat a little awkwardly and tried again. "What was it you wanted to see me about?"

He blinked and shook his head almost imperceptibly, and then the spell was broken. Only then did she realize she had been holding her breath. Slowly, and not a little unevenly, she released it.

"Right," Melbourne said. "I'm sorry. I was thinking about something else."

She nodded, but said nothing.

"I had the dream again Friday night, after I spoke to you. And again last night."

"Oh, yeah?"

"Yes. And on both occasions, it was a little different than it had been before."

"Did you see a face this time?"

He shook his head. "No. But there was more to it than there has been in the past."

"In what way?"

"God, where are my manners?" he said, suddenly seeming to remember something. He gestured toward the small couch beneath one window. "Sit down, Ms. Matheny, please."

Roxy did as he asked, placing her coffee mug on a side table as she watched him seat himself atop the desk a little to her left. With his sneakered feet dangling a few inches above the floor, his pose was casual but no less self-assured than it had been the Friday before in her office. Yet here, in this room, Spencer Melbourne seemed much more approachable. He didn't seem like a man who headed up a major corporation, didn't seem like the type to have attended a posh school like George Washington University, didn't seem like the kind of person who enjoyed an elitist activity like sculling on the Potomac at dawn.

He seemed like an average man who had average dreams and average desires. And she supposed, in a way, he was. Right now, all he wanted was to be reunited with a family he'd never known, something that no amount of education or wealth or power had enabled him to achieve for himself. For this basic desire to have a family—one shared by just about everybody on earth, she supposed—he had turned to someone average: Roxy Matheny. And for that reason, she suddenly didn't feel so average herself anymore.

"Your dream?" she reminded him when he made no move to continue.

He studied her thoughtfully for a moment, then nodded almost reluctantly. "For the first time, I knew where I was."

Roxy narrowed her eyes at him. "What do you mean?"

Melbourne scrubbed a hand through his hair, sighed heavily, then dropped it to his knee and absently rubbed the joint, as if the pain from an old injury were flaring up. "Before, when I've had the dream, I've never known where I was. I was just…somewhere. With someone. Everything was vague and indistinct." He met her gaze levelly before adding, "Except for the knowledge that the person I was with was my twin brother. That's the only part of the dream that's ever been definite."

Roxy pondered that for a moment, then repeated, "But this time you knew where you were."

He nodded once more. "In a way."

Again, he hesitated, and again she found herself waiting for his reply with unprecedented curiosity.

Finally, he told her, "I was in the backyard of an old house. It wasn't a house I recognized, but it was definitely the back-yard of a house. I saw a clothesline, a swing set and a red wagon turned on its side on the patio. It was amazing how much detail suddenly jumped out at me. I could even see the paint peeling in spots on the back of the house, and some rusty places on the wagon, and that the grass was overgrown and badly in need of mowing."

Roxy was skeptical. That really *was* a lot of detail to sud-denly spring up in a dream that had always been admittedly hazy. Still, she supposed it was possible that his simple act of sharing his dream with another human being for the first time might have opened some kind of psychological doorway in his brain. Maybe.

"You think what you were seeing was the house you lived in before you were adopted?" she asked.

This time he hesitated not at all. "I'm sure of it."

She still wasn't convinced. "How can you be so sure?"

His gaze never wavered from hers as he assured her, "I just am."

"Like you're sure you have this twin brother out there somewhere."

She could see his jaw clench tight and his eyes turn flinty. "Yes, in exactly that way."

Before she could say anything more, he leapt up from the desk and began to pace the small confines of the room. "Look, Ms. Matheny," he said without looking at her, "I get the feeling you're having a little bit of trouble believing me when I tell you the particulars of my situation. And call me crazy, but it seems to me that something like that might get in the way of your investigation."

Her eyebrows shot up in surprise at the vehemence of his charge. "No, it won't get in the way of my investigation."

He stopped pacing and spun around to glare at her. "Then you admit you don't believe me when I tell you I have a brother out there somewhere."

She lifted one shoulder in a shrug that was noncommittal. "I wouldn't say that exactly."

He moved to stand before her, his hands on his hips, his weight settled on one foot, staring down at her with those turbulent eyes. The position was one of utter authority, of complete assurance of one's rightness, and Roxy didn't like it one bit.

"Then what exactly would you say?" he demanded.

She bit her lip and willed herself not to buckle under his tone of command. Instead, she, too, stood, dropped her own hands to her hips and shifted her weight to her opposite foot, then stared up at him with eyes she hoped were equally turbulent. Her posture, even though it halted a good eight inches below his, appeared to surprise him, because he seemed to relax his stance some. However, he showed no sign of backing down any further.

"I'd say you're a guy who's used to getting his way," she told him frankly. "A guy who's got enough money and power to surround himself with yes-men and -women, and who, until now, has been able to buy or bargain for himself just about anything he's ever wanted. But now you want a family to replace the one you've lost, and you realize no amount of cash or clout will get it for you. And *I* think that might be clouding *your* judgment just a tad.''

He had narrowed his eyes at her while she spoke, and the color in his cheeks had heightened. Now his breathing began to come in a quick, raspy rhythm, and Roxy could see that she'd really ticked him off.

Well, too bad, she thought. She'd never been one to keep her thoughts to herself, and she couldn't see any reason to start now. Spencer Melbourne didn't seem like the kind of guy who wanted to be handled with kid gloves, anyway. She owed it to him to be honest with him. And the truth of the matter was, it was very unlikely that he was going to find himself a family when, in all likelihood, that family didn't exist.

"I see," he replied simply. "You think I'm imagining all this. That it's all some hopeless dream triggered by the deaths of my parents. That I'm just some pathetic, lonely man who hasn't got a hope in hell of ever being reunited with the only family he has left.''

Roxy sighed, and for the first time in her life regretted that she'd spoken so bluntly. What was it about Spencer Melbourne that brought out a sense of decency inside her she'd never known she possessed? Why did she suddenly want to take him by the hand and assure him that if anyone could find his family, it was Roxanne Matheny, P.I.? Why did she find herself wanting to pull his head down to her breast, to stroke his forehead with soothing fingers, to press her lips to his temple and—

It was those damned blue eyes, she told herself, halting the graphic images that formed in her brain before they could go any further. She'd always been a sucker for blue eyes, and Spencer Melbourne's were just about the dreamiest pair she'd ever seen. And now that they looked so hopeless and forlorn, she felt truly rotten.

Jeez, the guy probably already felt as if he'd been abandoned by his birth mother and the deaths of his parents, she reminded herself. Now she'd just added to it by telling him she thought his belief in the only family he had left was nothing but a pipe dream. And he was *paying* her, for God's sake. What kind of creep did that make her? What right did she have to dash his hopes before she'd even checked them out?

Just do your job, Roxy, she told herself. *It's what you're getting paid for. Don't let a guy rattle you just because he's good-looking and sexy and dreamy-eyed. You know you always wind up in trouble when you do.*

"Look, Mr. Melbourne," she began, hoping to somehow make amends for her behavior. "I apologize for what I said. It's not that I don't believe your family exists, it's just that I don't want you to get your hopes up about something that might not pan out."

"Why shouldn't I get my hopes up?"

His question stumped her. "What do you mean?"

"I mean, what's so terrible about getting my hopes up?"

"Well, just that you might be disappointed, that's all."

He shook his head. "Let me tell you something, Ms. Matheny. I'm *not* some pathetic, lonely man who needs your sympathy. You're missing the entire point. I *won't* be disappointed. My brother *is* out there somewhere. It's that simple. And it's why I hired you. Now if you aren't as convinced of that as I am, then I'm going to have to hire another private investigator to conduct this search."

She probably ought to call him on it, Roxy told herself. Retainer or no retainer, she still wasn't certain why she'd taken the case to begin with. Maybe it was because Melbourne's conviction that he did in fact have a twin brother out there somewhere hit a raw chord inside her. Maybe it was because she understood what it was like to want something— to want a family—that badly and know full well that it didn't exist.

How many times when she was a child had she made up stories for herself about a mom and a dad and a brother and a sister who loved her desperately and would never let her go? How many times had she lain awake at night waiting for someone to come looking for and find her? How many times had she nearly convinced herself that, as an infant, she'd somehow been separated from an all-American family who were worried sick about their missing little girl and doing everything they could to get her back?

And how many times had she had the hopes kicked right out of her by reality when nobody ever showed up?

Roxy had been a lonely kid. Her father had walked when she was still a toddler, and her mother had bolted a few years later. Roxy had been passed around from relative to relative until, at sixteen, she'd gone to spend a summer with her grandfather, Bingo. The two of them had recognized immediately that they were cut from the same cloth, that what made Roxy Roxy was exactly the same thing that made Bingo Bingo. Genetically speaking, they were two of a kind. And only then had she finally found a real home.

Such as it was. Her grandfather had been a man who wandered and kept odd hours, and as a result, Roxy had still spent a lot of time on her own. She'd still been a lonely kid. But at least there had been *someone* stable—kind of stable, anyway—for her to cling to in times of adolescent angst. Bingo had had answers for everything and a philosophy about life that, although a bit skewed, often made perfect sense. Maybe his answers hadn't always been accurate, but they'd always been comforting. For all his flamboyance and mischief, Bingo Matheny had been a good man. Roxy had loved her grandfather a lot. In many ways, she'd never loved anyone else.

Which was all the more reason she should keep Spencer Melbourne as a client, she decided. She understood where he was coming from in a way other investigators wouldn't. And maybe, in some weird way, taking on the search for his brother might help to exorcise the desire that still existed in her to find a family she knew she'd never have.

"It won't be necessary for you to find another investigator," she told him. "If anyone can find your brother, it's me. I give you my word."

Evidently, her assurance was satisfactory, because she could see his whole body relax. Of course, how could a woman not pay attention when a body like his was doing anything? Spencer Melbourne could make hosing out garbage cans look sexy. And why was she suddenly so preoccupied with thoughts of his anatomy, anyway?

Because you're a sap, she told herself. She'd been burned once by a guy like him, she reminded herself. Only an idiot would let something like that happen twice.

"There's just one more thing I request," Melbourne told her.

Roxy nodded. "Okay. What?"

"Actually, it's more of a demand."

She chewed the inside of her jaw for a moment, then told him, "I don't much care for demands."

"Too bad," he retorted. "Because I'm dead serious about this one."

"What is it?"

"I want to be instrumental in this investigation."

She wasn't sure she liked the sound of that. "Define *instrumental.*"

He strode slowly to the other side of the room and gazed at a photograph of himself and a senator from Virginia, the two of them standing in the middle of a river, each of them holding up a dead fish. Then he spun back around to look at Roxy. "I want to be kept informed of every step you take," he told her.

Was that all? "No problem," she assured him.

"I want to know what you're going to do before you do it."

"Like I said, no problem."

"Everything you find out, I want to know about it immediately."

"No problem."

"And I want to go with you wherever you have to go for this."

She opened her mouth to repeat her earlier assurances, but what came out instead was, "Problem."

"What?"

She met his gaze levelly. "I said, 'Problem.' Big problem. I won't agree to that."

"Why not?"

"Because I work alone, that's why."

He crossed the room again and stood before her, assuming the same proprietary posture he had held before. "Not this time, you won't," he told her.

"Oh, yes, I will," she countered.

"Oh, no, you won't."

"Look, Mr. Melbourne—"

"No, *you* look, Ms. Matheny. This is the most important thing I've ever undertaken in my life. And I won't entrust it solely and completely to someone who is, in effect, a total stranger."

"You said yourself that Bingo did some nice, discretionary work for your old man," Roxy reminded him. "And I told you that everything *I* learned, I learned from Bingo. *Discretion* is my middle name."

"I thought Prudence was your middle name."

"So I have two middle names. You rich people do that kind of stuff all the time. Sue me."

"Ms. Matheny—"

"I won't have you following me around everywhere I go. I just won't."

"Then you won't have me for a client."

She sighed in exasperation. "Any other P.I. is going to tell you the same thing," she stated. "No investigator wants a client tailing him all the time, asking questions and getting in the way."

"I promise you I won't get in the way."

"How do I know that?"

She wasn't sure, but she thought she saw a hint of a smile play over his lips before he told her, "I give you my word."

She was going to be sorry for this, she just knew she was. In spite of that, Roxy heard herself telling him, "All right. You can tag along. But the first time you do so much as step on my toe, you're banished back to the boardroom, get it?"

"Got it."

"Good."

He extended his hand to her, and reluctantly Roxy lifted

her own in return. Before she could make contact, he covered her hand with his, curling his fingers over hers in a manner that was in no way professional. His hand was warm and lively, his grip strong and self-confident. She could feel in his handshake that Spencer Melbourne was a man who wouldn't quit until he was completely satisfied.

And for some reason, that realization didn't reassure Roxy at all.

Three

———

"A Ms. Matheny to see you, Mr. Melbourne."

Spencer's attention shifted immediately from the communications system blueprint sitting on the desk before him to thoughts of the dark-haired, dark-eyed woman who was going to find his brother. He punched the button on his intercom and told his secretary to send her in.

Roxanne Matheny, P.I., was like no other person Spencer had ever met, casual to a point that stopped just shy of disorderly, frank-speaking to a point that stopped just shy of offensive. And utterly, thoroughly unimpressed by just about everything. Including Spencer Melbourne. In spite of all that, he found himself warming to her with every encounter he had with her. Perhaps it was precisely *because* she was so clearly unintimidated by him that he found her so agreeable.

Since the deaths of his parents, there had been no one around whom Spencer felt he could let down his guard. The majority of his acquaintances had been made through his work, and because all of them essentially worked *for* him as opposed to *with* him, he felt obligated to maintain an aura of professionalism. Even among those who weren't necessarily business associates, he held a certain notoriety and reputation. People in his social circle had known him virtually all his life as the son of a powerful, wealthy man, one who had become equally powerful and wealthy in his own right. And they responded to him with the deference men in his position were due, whether he wanted that deference or not.

Most people kept their distance, and those few who did manage to get close—even those women with whom he shared some dubious romantic entanglement—still approached him with an unmistakable attitude of awe. It wasn't a position Spencer was comfortable with. But it was one he was forced to uphold for business or social reasons, and simply because he knew of no other way to live.

There were a few in the upper echelons of his company with whom he could relax some, but even then, there was a definite corporate hierarchy with which he refused to tamper. He was the man in charge. Everyone who worked for him knew that. And because of that, it was impossible for him to ever be fully at ease around others.

Yet with Roxanne Matheny, he'd felt no obligation to reiterate his authority. Yes, she was working for him. Yes, he was paying her wages. And yes, she was answerable to him. But he was powerless to restrict her comings and goings. Nor did he have any desire to do so. Ms. Matheny had a job to do for him, and she was doing it. In that area, at least, she was the one in charge. Because of that, Spencer felt no compulsion to erect any kind of professional barriers between them.

That didn't prevent Ms. Matheny from behaving any way other than businesslike around him, however—something that Spencer felt oddly ambivalent about. Despite the knowledge that what the two of them shared was a working relationship, something in him responded to something in her that was decidedly less than professional. He wasn't sure exactly what was going on, just that there was something about Roxanne Matheny that defied his best efforts to keep things strictly official.

When she entered his office, she was dressed in baggy, man-styled, brown tweed trousers and an equally baggy, man-styled white shirt with a brown-and-black houndstooth vest hanging open over it. He half wondered if she'd left a felt fedora and trench coat sitting in a chair outside, wondered why she didn't carry a gold pocket watch like the ones the old Hollywood detectives had always seemed to consult. Perhaps she'd hocked it to buy more bullets, he thought before he could stop himself. Something about her getup just screamed *Sam Spade*.

"I'm sorry to just drop in like this," she told him. "But I was in the neighborhood."

"No apology necessary," he assured her as he rounded the front of his desk. He shook her hand briefly, then indicated a chair to his right, a superfluous gesture, because she had already moved to sit down in it. "What have you found out?"

She waited until he moved back behind his desk and took a seat himself. Then she told him, "I found out this isn't going to be as easy as I'd hoped."

Spencer frowned. "What do you mean? I thought you said missing persons was a piece of cake."

"Yeah, well, it was when Bingo was alive. He had this amazing collection of contacts and friends in high places. I thought they were *my* contacts and friends in high places, too, but a lot of them aren't nearly as willing to deal with me as they were with Bingo."

"Why not?"

"Evidently, my grandfather had a lot of inside information that he didn't get a chance to pass along to me."

"What kind of information?"

"Oh…like who's been sleeping with a congressman's wife—or with a congressman, for that matter—who's pocketed ten gees from his employer, who has kids fathered outside wedlock by highly respected foreign diplomats from countries who celebrate rigid morality…that kind of thing."

"Ah. I see."

"I guess extortion speaks a lot louder than longstanding friendship does."

Spencer tried to remain impassive. "Then how do we proceed?"

Roxanne Matheny crossed her legs and leaned back in the chair, wrapping the fingers of both hands around one knee. "You're not going to like it," she said quietly.

"Oh?"

She nodded. "Getting a copy of your adoption records and original birth certificate is going to be next to impossible."

Spencer told himself to stay calm. In his line of work, he'd learned long ago that there was no such thing as impossible. Besides, Ms. Matheny had said *next to* impossible. That meant there was still a way to get by whatever they needed to get by.

"Why impossible?" he asked.

Without altering her seemingly casual pose, she told him, "Normally, in this state, anyway, when someone wants to have their adoption records opened and find their biological parents, they have to get the permission of a circuit court— not local, circuit—to get a hearing with the state adoption board."

"Just to get a hearing?"

"Mmm-hmm. And even if you manage to get a hearing, it's unlikely you'll have much luck there."

"Why?"

"Because once you get that hearing, three judges will have to decide whether or not you have a good enough reason for wanting your records unsealed. And if you ask me, simple curiosity about a long-lost twin who might not even exist just ain't gonna cut it."

Spencer refused to accept her reasoning. No one could predict what a judge might decide. "What if it does? What if, for some reason, they do accept my reason for wanting the records unsealed?"

"Then you still might be out of luck. Prior to 1972, something called a 'writ of confidentiality' was included in adoption records. It was optional, but it was included when one or both of the parties involved requested it."

"And what does that mean?"

"It means that if the court unseals your records and finds one—whether it was signed by your birth mother or your birth father—then the record gets closed right back up again, and you don't get access to it in any way, shape or form." After a second's hesitation, she added, "Not unless there's some life-threatening illness involved that requires something like a bone-marrow transplant or something. So if one of those was signed, there's nothing we can do. Nothing legal, anyway."

"You said these writs were optional."

"Yeah, they were."

"So what if my mother or father didn't sign one?"

She eyed him dubiously, but replied, "Then there's a chance—a small one—that they might unseal the records. But I wouldn't count on it," she added hastily. "Like I said, you have to have a very good reason, and I'm not sure the courts would consider yours very good."

"But we still have a chance. A small one," Spencer conceded when he saw her about to object. "But still a chance."

She nodded reluctantly. "Yeah, there's a small chance. But then there's a small chance that the earth could go spinning out of its orbit and hurl itself into the sun, too."

He ignored her last comment and said, "Then do whatever you have to do to set the wheels in motion."

She sighed wearily. "I already have."

He was surprised at that, but said nothing.

Seeming to read his mind, she told him, "I figured you wouldn't let a small thing like a circuit court and three—count 'em, three—judges stop you. You just strike me as that kind of guy."

He wasn't sure if that was a compliment or not, so decided not to dwell on it.

"There might be some good news, though," she added when she saw his thoughtful pose.

"What's that?" he asked absently, still weighing his chances for success taking the judicial route.

"If your mother is dead and no father was named, they *might* release the information without too much quibble."

"Dead?" he repeated, snapped back from his reverie like a taut rubber band. For the first time, he realized that he hadn't given this whole thing nearly as much thought as he should have before he'd gotten into it. "You call the possibility of my birth mother's death *good* news?"

"Well, maybe not when you put it like *that....*"

"But I'm not even trying to find my mother," he argued. "I'm trying to find my brother. What if—"

She held up a hand to halt his objection. "I know. Like I said, petitioning the court to look for your mother is what we're *supposed* to do, the way the legal wheels normally turn. I didn't say it's what we're *going* to do. At least, not solely what we're going to do."

He told himself not to overreact, but still couldn't quite squelch the anxious sigh that erupted. "Would you mind clarifying that for me?"

"Like I said, I already filed the petition for you, but only as a formality. In the meantime, I'm also going to try to pull a few more strings. Bingo's not the only one who's made friends along the way. Mine are just of a less, um, a less influential...variety."

Spencer narrowed his eyes, not certain he wanted clarification on that. Evidently, however, Ms. Matheny took his expression to mean that he didn't trust her, because she clarified things for him, anyway.

"They're old boyfriends, all right? Nothing major, just...you know. I'll probably have to go out with one or two of them again. I'll have to make those no-bake chocolate-oatmeal-peanut-butter cookies for a couple of them." She dropped her gaze and lowered her voice some as she added, "I'll just, um, oh, ick. I'll have to talk baby talk to Doug...wear that stupid red bustier for Phil..."

Spencer couldn't help but smile. In an effort to ease her burden some, he confessed, "I love those no-bake chocolate-oatmeal-peanut-butter cookies. One of our cooks used to make them every Christmas."

He refused to comment, however, on the baby talk or the red bustier part. Something told him it was a bad idea to start

visualizing Roxanne Matheny modeling lingerie. He wasn't
sure, but he thought he saw her smile at his admission. When
she looked up at him again, however, her expression held
only calm neutrality.

"Ted, one of the cookie ones," she said, "works in the
same building where Family Court keeps all its old records.
For a couple dozen, I could probably get him to wander down
there during his lunch hour and accidentally look into a file
that's none of his business."

Spencer wanted to demand what on earth had possessed
her to ever go out with a man who had such easy morals,
then decided he was better off not knowing. Who Roxanne
Matheny dated was her business, not his. Unfortunately, he
wasn't quite able to completely squelch his curiosity about
her private life.

"So what happens then?" he asked.

"Let me get that far before we start worrying about anything else, okay?"

Reluctantly, he conceded. "Okay."

"I'll go by and see Ted now. See if he's still, um…" She
sighed fitfully. "See if he's still interested. In chocolate, I
mean." Before Spencer could ask, she added, "It won't be
necessary for you to come along on this trip. You'll just
cramp my style."

A bizarre image leapt up in his mind then, one of Roxanne
Matheny dressed in a skintight red dress, wearing three-inch
stiletto heels and a long strand of pearls, and clutching a five-
inch-long cigarette holder. As the image unfolded, he watched
her saunter into a room where an overworked, overwrought
file clerk was minding his own business, the lush tones of
"Melancholy Baby" blown from a sultry saxophone in the
background. He saw her sidle up next to the poor man,
watched as she cupped his hand in hers and flicked cigarette
ashes into his palm. Then this mental picture of Roxanne
Matheny bent the file clerk backward over his desk, buried
her fingers in his hair and covered his mouth with hers.

And then, for no apparent reason, the file clerk turned into
Spencer Melbourne.

Abruptly, Spencer halted the first reel of the low-budget *film noir* that was unrolling in his head, the one that cast Roxanne Matheny as the femme fatale and he himself as the sap. Not because he wasn't curious to see just how things between the two characters might turn out, but because there were just some things a man didn't want to think about.

Not yet, anyway.

Spencer scanned the back page of *The Wall Street Journal,* folded the newspaper neatly in half and eyed the woman seated beside him. He still wasn't sure why he had demanded to come along with Roxanne Matheny, P.I., on the search for his twin brother. God knew he had other things that demanded his attention far more insistently. A man didn't run a multi-national corporation by following around slight, dark-haired women who spoke and acted as if they were part of the back-drop in a Raymond Chandler novel.

But for some reason, Spencer had insisted. He told himself it was because he wanted to make sure she didn't do anything that would compromise him or botch the investigation. Be-cause he wanted to be sure she was as good as she'd assured him she was. Because he just wasn't absolutely certain he could trust her. As the days had passed, however, he had begun to wonder a bit about his motivation.

He had begun to wonder if maybe Roxanne Matheny hadn't been right in the assessment she'd offered of his life that first day in her office.

Not the part about him being lonely, of course. There was no way he was lonely. His life was fuller than anyone's. He had business and social obligations scheduled into the next century. He was almost always surrounded by people, and when he wasn't, he had dozens more only a phone call away. The mere suggestion that he was a lonely man was laughable.

It was the part about him being unfulfilled that bothered Spencer most. Was it actually possible that a man who had everything could still be unhappy?

Of course, he didn't have everything, he reminded himself. His twin brother was out there somewhere, waiting to be found. It was why Roxanne Matheny had entered Spencer's life to begin with, after all.

And she had been as good as her word. All week long, once she had discovered the particulars of his adoption that had occurred more than thirty-two years ago, she had kept Spencer informed of what she was doing, had alerted him to every move she intended to make in the search for his brother. And she'd let Spencer accompany her as she ventured into all the mysterious, dangerous places where a private investigator does her best work—to the Bureau of Vital Statistics, to the city archives, to the Department of Motor Vehicles, to the Library of Congress.

Spencer told himself he shouldn't be surprised that these were the places where detectives uncovered the things they needed to know. These places were, after all, data banks, and private investigators were looking for facts. Still, it had somewhat surprised him that he and Roxanne Matheny, P.I., hadn't had to venture into some seedy neighborhood wearing dark glasses and trench coats to disguise their true identities. And, if he forced himself to be honest, it had somewhat disappointed him, too.

And why that bit of whimsy had ever entered his brain was another mystery he'd have to have solved someday, more than likely by a psychiatrist instead of a private investigator.

Now, as he watched Roxanne Matheny sit before a microfiche machine, spinning through the pages of history, he was also beginning to wonder if his interest in this case was limited exclusively to finding his twin. An unprecedented—and unexpected—curl of delight had unwound in his midsection when his secretary had informed him Ms. Matheny had called this morning. And he'd been inordinately, and inexplicably, pleased when she'd asked him to meet her at the Library of Congress.

Why he should react in such a way mystified him. Not only had their outings been uncommonly boring, but Roxanne Matheny had offered no indication that she took any particular pleasure in his company. Not that he wanted her to take pleasure in his company, Spencer reminded himself. Why should he? Why should *she?* What the two of them had was a business arrangement. He was paying her to provide a service, and she was just doing her job. Whether or not the two of them enjoyed each other's company was immaterial.

Or, he told himself further, it should be. Unfortunately, for him, at least, that last aspect had become something of a preoccupation for him.

He noted the graceful way her fingers spun the knob back and forth, watched with interest the way her eyes scanned the quickly passing information. The stark-white flashing radiance of the ever-changing screen bathed her face in a fascinating array of light and shadow, and Spencer couldn't help but notice. On their initial encounter, he hadn't considered her to be a particularly attractive woman. Certainly he hadn't thought her *un*attractive, but she didn't claim the features of a traditionally beautiful woman. Now, however, he was beginning to think he had evaluated her appearance too hastily.

She had remarkably good cheekbones, high and sleek and aristocratic. Her eyes, the color of rich espresso, were wide and made more dramatic looking by dark, heavier-than-average eyebrows and lush, longer-than-average eyelashes. But it was her mouth that drew his attention most acutely. Originally, he had thought it too broad. Now, he considered it rather European. Full and expressive, with a lower lip that might wind up making another woman look pouty, on Roxanne Matheny, it suggested boundless sensuality. It was the kind of mouth that begged a man for a kiss, the kind of lower lip that a man would naturally draw inside his own mouth during such an embrace.

Spencer shuddered involuntarily and shook the realization off as soon as it occurred to him.

"Nope. Not a thing," she said, leaning back in her chair to throw him a look of commiseration.

He sighed wearily. Her ex-boyfriend's espionage had provided them with a copy of Spencer's adoption records, but the documents had offered little more than what he already knew. The only additional information had come in the form of the names of the attorneys involved, and the identification of the state-funded adoption agency that had orchestrated the arrangement. One of the attorneys had died six years ago. The other was retired and living in seclusion in the Cayman

Islands. So, for now, Roxanne had focused on the adoption agency to further their knowledge.

But the agency had released only what they termed "non-identifying information" about Spencer's parents. Now he knew that his birth mother had been a blue-eyed blonde, five foot seven, twenty-four years of age when he was born and employed as a grocery store cashier. She'd had no history of medical problems, and his birth had been uneventful. His father, he'd learned further, had been six foot one, with black hair and brown eyes, twenty-six years of age at Spencer's birth, also without any significant medical history, and had worked as a school custodian.

Good, solid people, gainfully employed. The salt of the earth. Why, then, had they given away their two young sons? Had they been unmarried at a time when marriage was socially essential for bringing a child into the world? Had theirs been an adulterous affair? Had there been family or financial problems? Or had they simply not wanted the burdens that came along with parenthood?

Spencer told himself they must have died. What other explanation could there be? And suddenly, without warning, he began to care about his absent parents as much as he did his absent brother.

Until he'd learned something about them, he hadn't wondered about his birth parents at all. Certainly at various points in his life, he had entertained some vague curiosity about the two people who had provided his genetic makeup. But he'd always considered his adoptive parents to be his real parents. His relationship with them had been loving and close, and there had been no reason for him to wonder too much about the people who had been physically responsible for his birth.

Too, Spencer had been so focused on finding his missing twin lately that he honestly hadn't given any recent thought to his birth parents. With the information provided by the adoption agency, he now had some inkling, some awareness of them, and he couldn't help but wonder what had happened to them, too. And strangely, the realization that they may be dead spawned a great deal of melancholy inside him.

Roxanne's voice brought him back to the present. "I can't find any announcement in any Virginia newspapers that twins were born on your birth date anywhere in the state. Nothing in Maryland or D.C., either.''

He roused himself from his musings, deciding some things were better dwelled upon when one was alone. ''Does that mean we have to start looking in other states?''

She shook her head. ''Not necessarily. It just means there was no public announcement of your birth, and now we're going to have to go back to being sneaky and underhanded to get information.''

''And where do we have to go for that?''

''Back to the adoption agency.''

''But they refused to reveal the names of my birth parents or the particulars of my birth. They also refused to give us access to my original birth certificate without a court order.'' He eyed her doubtfully. ''Did you happen to date someone who works for the adoption agency who'll steal my records in exchange for a night of tangoing?''

She shook her head again. ''Nope. But I know how to pick a lock better than anyone in the D.C. area. And that's saying something in this town,'' she stated unnecessarily.

This time Spencer was the one to shake his head. Vehemently. ''No. Absolutely not. I don't want to know about it if you're going to resort to something illegal like breaking and entering.''

''Hey, *you're* the one who told me you wanted to be kept informed of everything I do, everywhere I go,'' she reminded him. ''*You're* the one who wanted to come along on this expedition. I *told* you I didn't want you underfoot, but *noooooo*... You had to come along, anyway. And now that things are getting a little sticky, you want to back down like a sissy.''

She had dropped her gaze to the notebook on the table next to the microfiche machine, so he couldn't tell if she was joking or not. Still, calling a man a sissy—whether in jest or not—was tantamount to challenging him to a duel.

He narrowed his eyes at her. ''Who're you calling a sissy?''

She whiffled through the pages of her notebook, as if she were looking for some specific information. Almost absently, she told him, "I didn't say you were a sissy, just that you were backing down like one."

"I am *not* a sissy."

"Fine. You're not a sissy." When she glanced back up at him, her eyes were shining with merriment. "You got a black ski mask and some dark clothes?"

He stared at her for a moment, certain she was going to tell him she was just joking. When she did no such thing, he asked, "You actually expect me to come along with you on this thing?"

"*You* were the one who said you wanted to—"

"All right, all right." He growled inwardly. "I got myself into this. I guess it's my own fault. Where do you want me to meet you, and what time?"

She smiled at him. "My office. Friday night at eleven. That'll give me time to scope the place out and find out who comes and goes when." She wiggled her eyebrows playfully. "Be there or be square."

He sighed his reluctant agreement, then requested, "Just promise me one thing, Ms. Matheny."

"You might as well call me Roxy," she said. "We will be perpetrating a crime together, after all."

Her offer surprised him, but he found it oddly satisfying. "All right," he agreed. "Then you might as well call me Spencer."

She nodded. "Okay. So what's the promise?"

"Promise me that when they send me up the river you'll bake me a cake with a file in it."

Her smile grew broader. "Just tell me what flavor you like best. And don't complain when it comes out a little lopsided."

Lopsided, Spencer repeated to himself. Why did that word seem so utterly appropriate for his situation?

Four

"I still can't believe you talked me into this."

"I still can't believe you forgot your ski mask."

Roxy felt Spencer Melbourne's glare boring a hole into her back and spun around to return it in spades.

"You mean you were actually serious about that?" he asked her.

She shrugged. "I guess it's not that big a deal. If worse comes to worst, we can go out back and smear alley grime on your lily-white features." She glanced back down at the tools in her hands and, not quite under her breath, she added, "It might even do your system good to get a little dirty."

"Meaning what?" he demanded, his voice indicating he found no humor whatever in her suggestion.

"Nothing," Roxy mumbled. "Never mind."

She couldn't imagine what possessed her to keep baiting the too-too refined Mr. Spencer Melbourne. Probably the fact that he was just too-too refined, she immediately told herself in response. For the past week, every time she'd been within ten feet of the man, she'd been completely unable to think clearly. All she'd been able to manage were a few loosely gathered ideas about his case, and a lot of very clear imaginings about what it might be like to see Mr. Melbourne all mussed up and naked.

She expelled a restless sound when she realized she'd succumbed to such thoughts yet again. And, as she did whenever they occurred, she pushed them resolutely to the back of her mind where she knew they would simmer for a while before coming back to her full-blown. Probably while she was sleeping and could do nothing to stop them.

The man was just too handsome for his—or her—own good. Dressed in black jeans, a black turtleneck and black motorcycle boots, with a long day's growth of black beard shadowing the lower half of his face and his black hair falling free of its businessman-neatness, he looked like the kind of man Roxy would normally date. Tough and tumble, rough and ready. Unfortunately, in real life, he was none of those things. He was a pin-striped executive who was used to the finer things in life, one who had nothing in common with the likes of Roxy Matheny. The only reason he was with her now was because he was paying her lots of money and didn't quite trust her not to screw up the search for his brother.

Damn it all, she thought with an exasperated sigh.

She glanced at her watch. It was nearly eleven-thirty. By now the adoption agency office would be well and truly empty, the custodial staff having come and gone an hour ago. And although there was a rent-a-cop who patrolled the big office building, if Roxy timed things right—and she always did…well, usually, anyway—there was little chance she and Spencer would be interrupted in their excursion. In and out, she told herself. It shouldn't take more than fifteen or twenty minutes, as long as whoever took care of the files there had some basic knowledge of alphabetical order, and assuming she could find the right files once they got inside. ·

"I think I have everything we'll need," she said. "Let's go." She tucked her tools into the waistband of her black leggings at the base of her spine and yanked her black sweatshirt down over her hips. Her black, rubber-soled boots were silent as she strode to the door. As an afterthought, she turned to Melbourne again and asked, "You did bring gloves, didn't you?"

He made a wry face at her and pulled a pair of black driving gloves from his back pocket for her inspection.

She nodded her approval. "Then we're all set."

He shook his head. "I still can't believe you're actually going to go through with this. That *we're* actually going to go through with this."

Roxy relented some. "Look, it's not absolutely necessary for you to go with me. I just thought you'd want to make sure I did things the way you wanted them done. If you'd rather wait here until I—"

"No," he interrupted her. "I'll go. If you do get into trouble, it will be my responsibility, so I should be there."

She frowned at him. "If I get into trouble, it will be *my* responsibility, not yours."

"I'm the one who hired you," he reminded her.

"And I'm the one who's supposed to be doing my job the right way."

"But if something goes wrong, I'll—"

"Mr. Melbourne—"

"Spencer."

She hesitated for a moment, remembering that he had instructed her to address him that way, but still not sure it was such a good idea. With a sigh of exasperation, she continued, "Spencer, you want to tell me just what the hell is going on here?"

Her outburst seemed to make him forget whatever he was going to say. Instead, he only stared at her mutely, as if he had no idea what she was talking about. Finally, he asked her, "What do you mean?"

"I mean you've been acting like a mother hen ever since you hired me. You want to know what I'm doing and where I'm going, and what I'm doing going there to begin with. You say you're the one who's responsible for me and the outcome of this case when it's really the other way around.

And I can't figure out why you won't let me take that responsibility."

She shoved a fistful of dark brown bangs off of her forehead and eyed him wearily. "I've been doing stuff like this since I was a teenager, helping out Bingo in his investigations. You don't have to worry about me. I've never been caught. I'm good at what I do. You have my word I won't do anything to embarrass you or expose your search for your brother. Would you please just trust me?"

"I do trust you," he told her. "I just…"

"What?" she demanded.

He dropped his gaze to his hands and seemed to be making a great effort to concentrate on donning his gloves. "I just…" He hesitated again, then finally looked up to meet her eyes levelly. "I don't want you to get hurt, Roxy."

It was the first time he had addressed her by her given name, and she began to regret that she had suggested he call her that. She wondered why she had even extended the invitation for him to get so familiar to begin with. Something about the way he said her name made their relationship seem more intimate than it actually was. Made her feel as if a warm caress traveled over her entire body before settling over her heart. Made her want to hear him say her name over and over again in much the same way.

"I won't get hurt," she assured him. *Not by anything I'll encounter in the line of work, anyway,* she added to herself. *Except for maybe a particularly distracting blue-eyed client.*

"I'm still going with you," he said.

"Okay, then let's quit jawing and get out of here."

He tugged the door open for her and swept his arm out regally, silently requesting that she precede him through it. Roxy wasn't used to guys who did that kind of thing—who opened a door for another human being because it was the courteous thing to do. Usually, the guys she dated bolted through the door first. They also ordered dinner first, chose the movie or sporting event without consulting her and just generally made it known that they were the ones of most significant importance in the relationship.

Which pretty much explained why Roxy's love life was so nonexistent. There just weren't any decent guys out there. There were no men left who knew how to act in polite society. In short, all of the good ones were taken.

She shot a glance at Spencer as she approached him. Well, most of the good ones, anyway, she amended. Unfortunately, the few good ones left generally traveled well outside her own sphere of existence and wanted nothing to do with someone like her. Not that there was anything wrong with Roxy. She just doubted Spencer would be impressed by the compliment her grandfather had always paid her. She doubted he'd consider being called *a right broad* endearing, the way Roxy always had.

Spencer Melbourne would want a woman who'd come out wearing cotillion white gloves when she was sixteen, not one who'd been picking locks in black ones. He'd want a woman who could throw parties people would talk about for months, not one who could throw an adversary to the ground in a choke hold. He'd expect a lover to wear silk and lace, not Hawaiian print boxer shorts and a T-shirt that said My Mom Did Time At Quantico Federal Penitentiary And All I Got Was This Lousy T-shirt. And he'd doubtless want his mate to be feminine and submissive, not hungry and rabid, which was how Roxy was beginning to feel every time he was around.

Telling herself she was crazy to do it, she pretended to stumble as she passed him and grazed his chest with her shoulder. Yup, solid rock, she thought. Probably the only pinstriped executive in town who wasn't flabby and balding and boring. Why her? Of all the private investigators in all the neighborhoods in D.C., why did Spencer Melbourne have to come knocking on her door?

He reached out to steady her when she fell against him, even though she really didn't need steadying. She felt his fingers curl around her upper arms, pressing into her flesh with more familiarity than they had a right to. For one brief, brilliant moment, Roxy lifted her gaze to his and saw something in his eyes she was afraid to identify. For one solitary, scintillating moment, she thought she felt him move a little closer. For one warm, wishful moment, she thought he was going to kiss her.

Then he released her and dropped his hands to his sides and softly muttered, "Easy. Be careful."

Yeah, right, she thought.

She told herself she'd be wise to take his admonishment to heart. But then Roxy Matheny had never been one to follow orders very well. Even her own.

With a quick mental shake and roll of her shoulders, she exited her office and waited for Spencer to follow. Then, without a word, she locked the door behind them and headed for the bank of elevators at the other end of the hall.

And for some reason, when the elevator doors unfolded with an anemic *ding,* she couldn't help but think it terribly appropriate that she and Mr. Melbourne were going down.

The third time Spencer bumped his knee in the pitch blackness surrounding him, he decided he'd had enough. Where the hell was Roxy, anyway? And why did it feel so damned good to be thinking of her as *Roxy* now instead of *Ms. Matheny?*

He heard a soft whuffle of sound from the other side of the room and turned toward it. At the same time, Roxy's penlight flicked on, and he saw her at a file cabinet, checking the label on each metal drawer, her head bent intently toward her work. The soft glow of light surrounding her reminded Spencer of a portrait he'd seen in the National Gallery, one of a pre-Raphaelite Madonna. Roxy Matheny couldn't be any further removed from the object of that painting. In spite of that, and in spite of the fact that she was currently perpetrating a felony, she seemed more than a little heavenly to Spencer.

He had to stop thinking about her like that, he told himself. He was the last kind of man she should be interested in. Roxy Matheny was the sort of woman who should insist on a man who would love her to distraction and until the end of time. The distraction part Spencer figured he could probably handle with no trouble. The end of time thing, however, had always been a little hard for him.

Not that Roxy didn't deserve a forever-after kind of man. Spencer just wasn't that type himself. He'd been involved with enough women over the years to know that they only kept him interested temporarily. Once the newness of a relationship wore off, his attentions became easily diverted. Once the element of the unknown became the all-too-familiar, he was ready to put an end to it. That was just the kind of man he was. He was married to his work, and once he found his missing brother, he'd have all the family he needed or wanted.

Right now Roxy was a mystery, an enigma. She was like no other woman he'd ever met. But Spencer knew that if the two of them did become sexually involved, he'd eventually discover she wasn't so different from other women, after all. Eventually, he'd grow bored with the relationship and want out. And Roxy deserved better than that.

For that reason, if for no other, he knew he should keep his hands to himself. Unfortunately, thanks to that little stumble she'd had on her way out of the office, Spencer had discovered that his hands might have other ideas. He hadn't planned to reach out for her that way. She hadn't even lost her balance. But suddenly, he'd been holding her, and suddenly just holding her hadn't been enough. He'd wanted to kiss her. Badly. Only a massive countereffort had prevented him from doing so. But he wasn't sure he could mount an equally effective defensive the next time an opportunity like that presented itself. So he told himself to keep his distance.

"Jackpot," Roxy mumbled around the penlight she had stuck between her teeth. She withdrew a file from a drawer and held it up like a trophy.

Spencer's heart began to beat more rapidly at her announcement. "You found it? That's my adoption record?"

She removed the penlight from her mouth and turned it on her face, and he saw that she was smiling broadly. "Spencer Melbourne," she said in a mock baritone, extending the file toward him, "this is your life."

Just as he reached for the information in question, a loud *thump* sounded in the next room. Immediately, Roxy switched off the penlight, throwing them into utter blackness again. Spencer felt her fingers wrap in a manacle around his wrist and wondered how her eyes could have adjusted to the darkness so quickly. Then he had no time to wonder at all, because she was pulling him along forcefully behind her.

Just as he heard the soft *click* of a doorknob turning, Roxy jerked him to the ground behind a big piece of furniture. He fell atop her and instinctively rolled to his back, pulling her over him instead. She started to scramble off him, but the overhead lights flickered on above them, and she instantly ceased her movements. He saw that they had fallen behind a huge, oxblood Naugahyde sofa, and that they were safely out of view from whomever had come into the room. As long as that whomever stayed on *that* side of the room.

Spencer also saw that Roxy's eyes were huge and startlingly close, and that the black of her pupils nearly eclipsed the brown of her irises. Hers were the eyes of a woman who was aroused—there was no way he could mistake that. And helplessly, he swelled to life against her in response.

He knew at once that she felt that response, because her eyes grew even wider and her breathing became erratic. Her breasts rose and fell rapidly against his chest as she tried to keep her breathing silent, and her cheeks warmed with red. She licked her lips and closed her eyes, and Spencer gripped her more tightly against him.

On the other side of the sofa, someone was whistling "*Malagueña*" as they made their way to the door on the other side of the room, the one that opened onto a back stairway that ultimately led to the outside. The someone rattled the knob to check the lock that Roxy had picked scarcely ten minutes ago, the one she had deftly relocked once she and Spencer were inside. Then the someone strode easily back to the other side of the room again, flicked off the light and closed the door, locking it on their way back out.

The entire episode lasted less than a minute. But Spencer felt as if he'd just gone ten sets on the handball court. His heart pumped blood through his body at a rate to rival any race car's, and his skin felt alive all over. There was a beau-

tiful woman lying on top of him, one who was responsible
for this feeling of being more alive than he'd ever been before. She was soft and warm and clearly as aroused as he.
Utter blackness enveloped them. So Spencer did the only natural thing he could do. He kissed her. Hard. The way he had
wanted to for days.

For a few delirious seconds, she kissed him back. Then she
seemed to think better of the action and shoved herself away
from him. In the darkness, Spencer could hear her breathing
become thready, could feel her hands gripping his shirt in two
tight fists, could sense her indecision. And shamelessly, he
took advantage of her ambivalence. Instead of letting her
make the choice on her own, he decided to do his best to
bring her around to his way of thinking. He pushed himself
up on his elbows and reached for her again, pulling her back
down against him to kiss her. This time, when he covered her
mouth with his, he took possession. This time, he made sure
she knew he had no intention of letting her go.

Then, without warning, Roxy responded. She buried her
fingers in his hair, covered his mouth with hers and straddled
him. She rubbed herself insistently against him, crushed her
pelvis against his own and stifled a groan. Unable to tolerate
being so dominated, Spencer rolled until she lay beneath him
again, settled his weight between her legs and ground his hips
against hers. Then he dragged his open mouth along her throat
and tugged at the neck of her sweatshirt. When it wouldn't
give and allow him access to the prize he sought, he shoved
his hand under the waistband instead.

Only then did he remember that he was wearing gloves,
but impatience and the hazy recollection that he was in the
middle of committing a crime prevented him from removing
the dark leather coverings. He skimmed his gloved fingers
over each of her ribs, and she sucked in her breath at the
foray, tugging his lower lip into her mouth to kiss him more
hungrily. The sensation of having her so consume him drove
Spencer to explore her more eagerly, more hastily, more
intimately.

Without ceremony, he unhooked the front closure of her
brassiere when he encountered it and covered her breast with
his leather-clad hand, palming it to life. Beneath the thin layer

of his glove, he felt the stiff peak ripen between his thumb and forefinger, and he lowered his head toward it, tracing eager circles with his tongue before covering the warm flesh entirely with his mouth. He squeezed her breast in his hand to give him fuller access to her nipple, and felt Roxy arch against him with a strangled sound. Yet she made no move to stop his exploration.

Instead, she tangled her fingers in his hair more tightly and pulled him closer. Then slowly, she pressed her hands down the length of his spine, covered his buttocks with both hands and urged him more forcefully between her legs. Spencer could almost swear he felt her heat and dampness sinking into his own clothes, and he wanted nothing more than to sheathe himself deep inside her. He thrashed wildly against her, over and over again, halting only when he realized the madness of his actions. Finally, some semblance of coherent thought entered his brain, and he remembered where they were and what they were supposed to be doing.

"We have to get out of here," he gasped. "Now."

He felt Roxy nod against his shoulder and somehow managed to get to his feet. He fumbled for her hand and tugged her up behind him, tucking the pilfered file folder under his other arm. Neither of them spoke as she crept to the door, unlocked and opened it, then relocked it again behind them. They remained silent as they made their way effortlessly down the stairs and through the parking lot behind the building, and he pretended not to notice when she reached beneath her sweatshirt to refasten her brassiere. Wordlessly, they trudged the half mile back to Roxy's car and climbed inside.

Only then did Spencer dare venture a glance in her direction. And only then did his heart rate increase again. In the pale bluish light of a street lamp overhead, he could see that her cheeks were still red. Not from the flush of heated desire, but from the scrape of his rough beard. When she turned slightly toward the light, he saw that high on her cheek she carried an angry red abrasion that would probably stay with her for days, and the knowledge that he had so marked her burned inside him. Her hair was tangled, half out of the stubby ponytail she'd been wearing, and the neck of her sweatshirt was torn a good three inches. She had a bite mark on her throat. And her chest still rose and fell in rapid succession.

He had no idea he'd been so rough with her. But instead of feeling guilty about the realization, he became more aroused. Only now, he wanted to make it up to her for being so quick to attack. Now, he wanted to take her in his arms and kiss her languidly, patiently, gently. He wanted to lie down beside her and stroke with utter care every soft curve on her body. He wanted to caress her and pet her and take days to do it. He wanted to taste her leisurely and explore her thoroughly. Next time, he thought, he would do just that.

Next time.

"I'm sorry," he said softly.

He hadn't meant to apologize, but the words erupted just the same. He really wasn't sorry for what had happened. But he was sorry he had been so rough. Something in Roxy Matheny just brought out the beast in him. And, truth be told, he had kind of enjoyed experiencing that side of himself, as startling as it had been to discover it existed. That was no excuse, however, to behave like an animal with a woman who deserved so much more.

"It's okay," she told him quietly.

But he could tell by the tone of her voice that it wasn't okay at all.

"I didn't mean to hurt you," he told her.

She shook her head. "You didn't hurt me. It's not that."

"Then what?"

"Just drop it, okay?" She stared straight ahead, out the windshield, but she didn't seem to be seeing anything at all. "Let's just forget it happened, all right?"

"Roxy—"

"Just drop it."

But Spencer wasn't quite ready to do that. Instead, he risked inflaming the situation further by stating flat out, "I had no idea danger could be such a strong aphrodisiac. Nothing like that has ever happened to me before. I didn't mean to take advantage of you like that. I just—"

"*You* took advantage of *me?*" she demanded.

When she turned to look at him, he could see by the look in her eyes that she, too, had been more than a little overcome by the animal inside herself. There was something feral and untamed flickering in her eyes, some leftover wildness from their recent encounter that hadn't quite yet been extinguished.

"Roxy, I—"

"No, don't say anything," she insisted.

She held up her hand palm out, in a halting gesture, and he realized for the first time that she was trembling. An all-over tremble that shook her entire body. He reached for her, to pull her close, to warm her in whatever way he could, but she easily pushed him away.

"What happened back there…it just happened," she told him. "It didn't mean anything. It was just the result of a weird situation. There's no reason to read anything into it. So let's just forget about it. Okay?"

Still Spencer refused to let it go that easily. There was no way he was going to brush off what had happened as meaningless. But he wasn't sure he was ready to explore the matter to its logical conclusion, either. If there even *was* a logical conclusion.

"Okay?" she repeated when he didn't reply.

"Okay," he agreed reluctantly. But he qualified his response by adding, "For now."

Roxy opened her mouth to say something more, but Spencer covered it lightly with his fingers. His action surprised her into silence, so he dropped his hand and leaned toward her, touching his mouth to hers, this time with a gentleness and tenderness completely at odds with the reckless passion that had overtaken him before. He brushed his lips softly over hers, then trailed the tip of his tongue gingerly across her lower lip. Her eyes fluttered closed for a moment, opening only when he pulled away.

"For now," he repeated softly. "But this isn't the end of it, Roxy. Not by a long shot."

Five

"**W**ell, I'll be damned." Roxy rubbed her tired eyes, then glanced down at the file on her desk once again. The information was right there in black-and-white—well, black and aged, somewhat faded yellow—and Spencer had assured her all along that it was true. Nevertheless, it still surprised her to see it.

On the battered leather sofa on the other side of her office, Spencer jackknifed into a sitting position. He still wore the trappings of their earlier, felonious outing, still looked dangerous and treacherous and way too sexy. For about the millionth time, Roxy had to tamp down the memory of their embrace during the break-in, force herself not to think about exactly what had happened scarcely an hour ago.

Unfortunately, a warm ripple of delight still wound through her when she recalled the way his leather-clad hand had felt rubbing along her flesh, and the mind-scrambling sensations wreaked by the grinding of his pelvis against hers. Delicately, she fingered the torn fabric of her sweatshirt and brushed her thumb over the tender red spot high on her cheek. And she marveled again at the explosive quality of Spencer Melbourne's lovemaking.

You always had to look out for the quiet, boy-next-door types, she reminded herself. The guys who played by the rules in life were always the ones who went crazy behind closed doors. At least, that's what she'd always heard.

The episode had ended as quickly as it had begun. They'd returned to her office in silence, and Spencer had dropped onto the sofa without a word. Roxy had picked up the file folder he'd tossed, ignored, onto the sofa and had dropped it onto her desk instead. She'd asked him if he wanted to look at it first. She'd been surprised when he'd shaken his head and told her no. Instead, he'd lain down quietly and covered his eyes with his forearm, as if he didn't want to know the particulars of his past. As if he were afraid of what he would discover about himself.

But at her quiet remark, he now sat rigidly at attention, his gaze steely blue and coldly unwavering, his fisted hands white-knuckled and pressed against his thighs. "What?" he asked softly. "What is it?"

Roxy tried to smile reassuringly, but the gesture fell a little short. "You were right," she told him. "You really do have a twin brother."

Spencer stared at her mutely for a moment, then all the air seemed to leave his lungs in a quick *whoosh*. He dropped his chin to his chest and splayed his hands open over his knees. Every muscle in his body relaxed. Only then did Roxy realize that he hadn't been quite as certain about his brother's existence as he'd let on. Only then did she realize that he'd instigated this search as much to reassure himself as he had to find his missing twin.

"I thought I was the one who was supposed to be so incredulous," she said quietly.

He shook his head slowly but didn't look up. "You can't imagine what this means to me," he said. He sounded weary and nearly stretched to the limit. "You have no idea what I've been going through for the past few months. How often

I've wondered if…" His voice trailed off before he completed the sentence.

"If what?"

He buried his head in his hands, clenching his dark hair in fisted fingers. But he didn't answer her, and Roxy didn't press the issue. He was right about one thing. She couldn't imagine what he was feeling right now. She had no idea what it would be like to discover you had a past you had never known about before. Or how it must be to find out that such an intense desire for a family that might not exist was about to be fulfilled. She couldn't imagine how it must feel to know you weren't alone in the world, after all.

"If maybe I was losing my mind," Spencer finally said.

When he looked up, his eyes were heavy lidded and damp. He rubbed them fiercely, then stood and began to pace a slow circle around the small office.

"I lied to you, Roxy," he told her as he moved restlessly about. "I wasn't absolutely certain that I had a twin brother out there. I thought I was, but until you said that…" He paused in his pacing and turned to face her fully. "I realize now that I wasn't so certain, after all. Now that I do know for sure, it's like…it's like someone opened a window to allow light and freedom to a room where I've been trapped in the dark for months."

He strode cautiously closer to her desk, but still made no move to look at the file. "I realize now that part of me was afraid that maybe I *was* just making up a missing brother. That maybe I was hallucinating or delusional or something. That I was just creating this fantasy twin to fill an emotional void opened up by the loss of my parents. You were right, Roxy. I was a lonely guy. But now…"

"Now you won't have to be lonely anymore," she supplied for him when he didn't complete the statement. "At least, you won't have to be once we locate your brother."

The look he gave her then made her squirm. It wasn't an unpleasant look, nor an unpleasant sensation for that matter, just…odd. Roxy wasn't sure what to make of it. So she decided to just ignore it, and hoped maybe that would make it go away.

"Can I see?" Spencer asked, extending a hand halfheartedly toward the file folder on her desk.

"Sure." She spun it around so that the information was facing him and shuffled through a few pages. "See? Here on your original birth certificate, in the space that asks if yours was a multiple birth, the box marked *twin* has been checked."

He picked up the document in question between his thumb and forefinger, holding it gingerly, as if it were an ancient manuscript that he feared would blow away in a swirl of dust if he handled it too roughly.

"Sherry McCormick," he murmured softly.

Roxy eyed him curiously. "What?"

"That was my mother's name," he said, not looking up. "My birth mother, I mean. Sherry McCormick. And my father was James McCormick. They were married."

Roxy moved to the front of her desk and stood beside Spencer, reading over his shoulder. "So they were," she said softly.

"And the name they gave me when I was born was Stephen James McCormick."

Roxy bit her lip and remained silent. For the first time, she understood that there was a lot more to Spencer's quest than a missing brother. She had overlooked the fact that he might be just as curious about his parents. And about himself. Anyone in a similar situation would be, she supposed.

She didn't remember her own folks particularly well, but that hadn't kept her from wondering what they had been like. All the reports she'd received from her relatives indicated that her mother and father had been wild and immature and grossly irresponsible. She had preferred to think of them as the impulsive bohemian types instead. Still, it didn't change who she was today.

"Stephen James McCormick," Spencer repeated. "Stephen McCormick. Steve McCormick." He turned to look at Roxy. "What kind of person do you think of when you hear the name 'Steve McCormick'?"

She paused for a moment, giving his question a lot of thought. "I think...I think Steve McCormick would probably be the kind of guy who worked in a middle-management position somewhere. Like maybe for an automotive manufacturer. He'd be married to a woman named Susan, or maybe Carol, and they'd be celebrating their tenth anniversary this year."

She thought some more before she continued. "I can see Steve and Susan-or-Carol with three kids—two boys and a girl—and Steve would be the little league coach for the younger boy's team. He'd be trading off carpooling with his wife, running his kids to band practice, ballet lessons and summer camp, and he'd take an occasional antacid to get through the day. He'd watch pro sports on TV, think a lot about how he really should start jogging, and he'd love hot, open-faced roast beef sandwiches and macaroni and cheese."

Spencer looked back down at his birth certificate and stroked the pad of his forefinger slowly over his original name. Then he smiled at her character profile. "Do you think Steve McCormick would be a happy man?"

Roxy nodded. "Yeah. I think he'd be real happy."

Spencer's smile grew a bit sad. "I think so, too."

She wasn't sure where he was headed with this conversation, but she was willing to do her part to contribute. "So you think you would have liked growing up as Steve McCormick?"

He opened his mouth to respond, closed it, then opened it again. But still, no words emerged. Finally, he turned to gaze at Roxy, and she didn't think she'd ever seen anyone who looked more lost and confused.

"If I had grown up as Steve, I never would have been Spencer."

"No, that's true."

"I never would have met my parents, whom I loved more than you can possibly know."

"That's true, too."

"I wouldn't have met a lot of the people that I know now."

"There's a good chance you wouldn't have met any of them."

"I might be a completely different man."

"You might be."

He sighed, a shaky, uncertain sound. Then he looked at his birth certificate again. "There's nothing in here about my twin," he said softly. "Other than the fact that I do have one."

"That's because this is *your* birth certificate," Roxy told him, "not your brother's. His adoption was obviously handled separately, but probably by the same agency. Unless we know what his name is now, though, we'd have to pull every record they have to find him."

"Then how are we going to find him?"

"We can trace him through your birth parents."

"How?"

"Now that we have their names and know that you were born in Virginia, it will simply be a matter of going to the Bureau of Vital Statistics and checking the records. Piece of cake," she added with a halfhearted snap of her fingers. "Just like I promised."

Spencer nodded. "Will you be able to find out what happened to my parents, too?" he asked. "Whether or not they're still…"

"I can find that out, too," she told him. "If you want me to."

"I want you to."

"No problem."

For a long moment, he continued to stare at the birth certificate in his hand, the pad of his thumb first covering, then revealing, then covering again, the name he had been given at birth. Roxy had no idea what he was thinking about. But she could see that he was confused. And she couldn't help but wonder if maybe what had occurred between them earlier that evening was a part of that confusion. And she wondered why she cared.

Just as she turned to move back behind her desk, Spencer

reached over and wrapped his fingers loosely around her wrist.

"Roxy?"

She spun slowly back around to face him. His eyes were bluer and clearer than she'd ever seen them, and she thought that if she wasn't careful, she might just drown in their depths. "Yeah?"

"Thanks."

She smiled, then shifted her hand to weave her fingers with his, giving them a light squeeze. "No problem, Spencer," she assured him quietly. "Just doing my job."

Roxy discovered the fate of his parents that night, immediately after he left her office to go home. The whole sordid story was there in his file, but Spencer had been so wrapped up in memorizing the facts on his birth certificate that he hadn't even bothered to look at the rest of the information stacked inside the manila folder. Maybe it hadn't occurred to him that there would be so much available for his inspection and, for that reason, hadn't bothered to investigate the contents further. Or maybe he just hadn't wanted to know yet.

In either case, Roxy didn't approach him with her discovery until almost a week later. She kept her distance from Spencer for a lot of reasons that week. For one thing, she was somewhat stalled on the case and not entirely certain what would be the most effective way to go about finding the lost McCormick twin. Although she knew enough now to launch an effective search, she wasn't certain what the best strategy would be. For another thing, she thought Spencer might need a little time to absorb everything he'd already learned about himself before she dumped the rest of his family history into his lap.

But most of all, Roxy kept her distance because she needed time to think herself. And not just about the case, either. She still needed time to figure out just what the hell had happened between the two of them during the break-in. She still needed time to figure out what on earth had come over her that night.

Okay, maybe she already knew that. She was lonely. She'd

admit that readily. It had been a long time since she'd been with anyone, especially anyone with the looks and prowess of a man like Spencer Melbourne. She was a normal woman, with normal desires. And she wasn't so stupid that she didn't take advantage when an opportunity presented itself. Or, more accurately, when one wound up sprawled on top of her, ripe and eager, and kissing her as if she was the answer to a prayer.

But she wasn't so stupid that she was going to open herself up for a fall, either, and that's exactly what Spencer represented. If he were some other guy, some guy who had *something* in common with her, she might actually take a chance on letting things develop naturally between them.

But Spencer Melbourne wasn't some other guy. He was like no man she had ever met before, a man she wasn't likely to forget. Ever. She knew that was why she couldn't stop thinking about him, and she knew that was why she should put a stop to whatever was developing between them. She didn't want to end up alone and empty, wondering about a man she would never see again, a man who was more concerned with appearances and opportunities than he was about a woman who loved him. Roxy had been down that road before. It was no fun. And she had no intention of ever going there again.

But she was running out of excuses to put Spencer off. And she had no choice now but to approach him with the things she had uncovered in his adoption records. She just wasn't sure how he was going to take all the news once he heard it.

So she'd decided to break it to him gently. She figured it might be best to meet early in the morning at his place, before he went to work, at a time when he was alone and away from the distractions and responsibilities of his office. Then, once he listened to what she had to reveal, he could fall apart in private. But when she called to make the appointment late that afternoon, Spencer insisted on seeing her immediately instead.

Now she stood across the street from his home and listened

to the rumble of her empty stomach. Although she suspected he had grown up in a big, rambling house in the well-heeled suburbs of Falls Church or Alexandria, Spencer now occupied a place in Georgetown. It was a red brick town house near the university, far from the shops and clubs of M Street, on a tree-lined, cobblestone avenue where life was a bit more quiet.

Across the street from his town house and directly behind Roxy was a small park, its lush oaks and maples stained with red and gold and orange now that autumn was in full swing. A rowdy group of toddlers, tended by their nannies, squealed with every bump of the teeter-totters and shouted heartily as they clambered up and down the jungle gyms. Roxy paused on the other side of the tall, wrought-iron fence surrounding the park to observe the children for a moment and smiled involuntarily at their antics.

"Roxy!"

Her name erupted from behind her at the same time a cool breeze swept her hair away from her neck and over her face. She brushed the dark tresses aside as she spun around, only to see Spencer standing framed by his front door on the other side of the street. He still wore his work clothes—this time an impeccable slate gray suit accented with a matching tie and handkerchief in amethyst—and she bit her lip at the way her heart began an erratic tattoo against her breastbone.

Almost involuntarily, she began to walk toward him, only remembering as an afterthought to watch for traffic when she came to the street. Somehow, it seemed as if she had no choice but to go to him, whether he had called out to her or not. Something in him compelled her. Regardless of the differences in their backgrounds and their life-styles, there was something in Spencer Melbourne that spoke with quiet urgency to something in her. And she was helpless not to respond. When she stood before him, his gaze met hers, and she could see immediately that he was troubled.

But instead of asking her right out why she had wanted to see him, he levered his gaze over her shoulder at the park across the street, where the children still screeched and laughed and chased one another about.

"They're fun to watch, aren't they?" he asked softly, evidently having caught her in her earlier observance of the scene.

Roxy threw a quick glance over her shoulder, smiled at the children, then turned back to Spencer. "Yeah, I guess so. From a distance, anyway."

"You don't like kids?" He continued to stare past her at the rambunctious children.

She shrugged. "They're okay. As long as they belong to someone else. I've never much considered myself to be the maternal type. And seeing as how I'm not exactly on intimate terms with any kids, I really can't say too much about them."

"I like kids." His tone was thoughtful, distant. "Sometimes, after I've had an especially rough day at work, I'll look down at that park from my bedroom window and just watch those kids running around. They're so full of energy, so happy...so oblivious to what the world is really like. They're so caught up in enjoying the moment, that it never occurs to them..."

His voice trailed off, and Roxy wondered what he had been about to say. Instead of completing his sentence, however, he just shook his head and smiled sadly. "I bet none of them wonders about who he really is."

He was silent for a moment, then finally dropped his gaze back to her face. "What is it?" he asked. "What have you found out?"

She was a little disappointed that the conversation took such a turn, but was reluctant to pry further. Whatever was going on in Spencer's head was none of Roxy's business. That didn't stop her from being curious about him, of course. But it did demand that she return to their earlier, more professional demeanor.

She inclined her head toward the foyer behind him. "Can we go inside?"

He nodded quickly, only then seeming to realize they were standing out on his front porch—not a particularly good place to be having a meaningful conversation. He stepped aside and swept his arm toward the interior of the house, in much the same way as he had done at her office that night a week ago.

Had it really been just a week? she wondered as she stepped inside. For some reason, it seemed so much longer.

Spencer's house was very much like Spencer, she noted, elegantly appointed with deep, compelling colors, and obviously very expensively decorated. It was crowded with antiques and artwork, the furnishings fine and the lights low. Whimsically, Roxy thought it was the kind of place that should be featured in a magazine with a name like *Incredibly Rich People Today* or *Man, Has This Guy Got Taste*.

Strangely enough, however, his house was in no way formal. The furniture was old and obviously well-used. A scattering of magazines were strewn haphazardly atop the coffee table. Photographs littered the mantel at odd angles. A coffee cup sat neglected on one end table, a curl of steam rising above it. This was obviously a house that was lived in. And Roxy felt comfortable and very much at ease inside it.

Until she spun around in the center of the living room and saw her host gazing at her with a posture that was anything but easy. She wasn't sure what his expression meant, but Spencer seemed in no way comfortable. She supposed she couldn't blame him. His was an awkward position to be sure. For the past week, he had been straddling two life-styles— one that was and one that might have been. By a simple twist of fate, he had ultimately become someone destiny might never have intended him to be. Instead of Steve McCormick, he was Spencer Melbourne, the two identities entirely unrelated. Roxy could only begin to wonder how that must feel.

Spencer sighed restlessly and wished he could figure out what was causing the fiery knot in his stomach to rage hotter than it had been all week. Any number of things, he supposed. It could be the result of the utter confusion he'd been feeling about his identity since leaving Roxy's office last Friday. Or it could be because of his fear of what was to come. Maybe it was just caused by the fact that he couldn't stop thinking about Roxy, and all the things he wanted to do to her and with her.

Or maybe it was just his sudden realization that his perception—about everything—was becoming totally skewed.

For example, he had never much paid attention to the way his house was furnished until Roxy stood smack-dab in the center of his living room. His father had purchased the Georgetown town house before Spencer's arrival and had always used it on those occasions when the elder Melbourne had worked late or needed to be in early, making the commute from Falls Church difficult.

Back then there had been no metro making the trip into D.C. a quick hop. In spite of that new convenience, however, Spencer hadn't had any desire to live in the house where he'd grown up and had sold it after his parents' deaths. By then he'd already been living in the Georgetown house, anyway, having used it as a full-time residence since he'd taken over his father's position at Melbourne Communications Systems upon the old man's retirement. And by that time, he'd been so familiar with the place that he honestly hadn't paid much attention to its appearance.

Until now. Until he saw Roxy Matheny standing amid all that fine antique furniture. She was dressed in vivid red leggings and a knee-length sweater the same shade, with a long yellow scarf looped loosely around her neck. Brightly colored, shiny wet autumn leaves clung to her unwieldy hiking boots. Her dark curls tumbled wildly around her face and shoulders, and her cheeks were pink from the burr of the cold air outside.

She looked like an exotic jungle blossom that should be growing wild and free, confined instead to the even, organized rows of an artificially lit hothouse. Something about a vibrant, vivacious Roxy amid all that old, drab furniture just didn't sit well with Spencer. But for the life of him, he couldn't put his finger on why.

Maybe it was because she didn't look as if she belonged here. And maybe it was because he was beginning to wonder if he belonged here himself.

"Drink?" he asked suddenly as he moved to the collection of crystal decanters that sat on the cherrywood secretary in the corner of the room.

"No, thanks," she told him. But she followed him in that direction, anyway.

"I will, if you don't mind," he said as he decanted the Scotch and half-filled a matching crystal tumbler. "Something tells me I might need it."

"No problem. It's your place, after all."

His place, he thought. Was she trying to tell him something? Like maybe he should stay in his place and she should stay in hers? Or, as usual, was Roxy's presence just muddying his thoughts so much that he wasn't sure what the hell was going on?

"This is a beautiful house," she added, running her fingers gently over the sleek reddish wood of the secretary. "You have some lovely things."

Spencer had heard that comment on a number of occasions, but the remark had usually been punctuated either with a hint of disdain or a touch of jealousy. With Roxy, it sounded like what it was—a simple statement of fact. There was no envy, no scorn for his wealth, in her words. She was simply making an observation. And he appreciated it.

"Thanks," he said as he recapped the bottle and lifted the glass to his lips for a quick sip. The heat of the liquor soothed him some, but having Roxy so close quickly agitated him again. "My mother decorated the place for my father years ago. It's really more a reflection of them than it is of me."

"It's still nice. What's that?"

She pointed at something in the secretary, and without even turning around to look at what she was indicating, he knew what she was asking about. There were only two things housed behind the beveled glass doors—books and a teddy bear. Rare, first - edition, leather - bound, author - inscribed, antique books, and a black - and - brown, one - eyed, tattered- to - the - stuffing, stitched - and - restitched - and - restitched- again teddy bear. The former had been painstakingly acquired by Spencer's father. The latter had always belonged to Spencer. It was an eyesore and an icon. It was Spencer Melbourne's legacy.

"That," he said, "is Steve McCormick's life. His name is Charley. He's all that's left of what came before my parents adopted me. My mother told me I was clinging to him in the crib in the orphanage nursery, and that I refused to turn loose of him come hell or high water. He's the only thing they brought with me that was mine before. He's been with me, I suppose, since day one."

Roxy eyed the bear contemplatively, but Spencer had no idea what she was thinking about. Probably something along the lines of how ridiculous it was for a grown man to keep a ragged toy under glass like a priceless gem. He supposed he could explain to her exactly how important that bit of lint and stuffing was to him, but he wasn't sure she'd be able to understand. Not because she wasn't sympathetic, but because he wasn't too sure of the attachment himself.

Oh, it was probably natural to cling to the only item that predated his only known identity. But really, he was an adult now and had put his life before adoption behind him. Hell, he couldn't even remember what his life before adoption had been like. A few vague dreams meant nothing. And the teddy bear was literally falling apart at the seams.

But he'd clung to Charley in those early years, and in many ways, he clung to him still. The bear was a reminder that there was more to Spencer than he knew—more than anyone knew. And Charley was a reminder that there was someone else out there like him. Someone who might possibly own a teddy bear very much like that one. And whether it was housed in a Georgian cherrywood secretary worth thousands of dollars or stashed in a cardboard box in a dilapidated, damp garage, Spencer didn't care. The bear was his link to his brother. It was the most valuable possession he owned.

"What have you found out?" he asked, spinning toward Roxy and shoving thoughts of Charley aside.

As if she only now remembered that she was carrying it, she withdrew the manila folder tucked under her arm and extended it toward him. He recognized it immediately as his adoption record, but for some reason, he had no desire to take it from her. For some reason, he was suddenly unwilling to uncover anything else about himself.

"There's a lot of stuff in here you didn't see last week," she told him softly.

He met her gaze levelly. "I know."

"A lot of stuff that you really need to look at."

"Okay." But still, he made no move to accept the record from her.

Her expression grew puzzled, and she lowered the folder slowly to her side. "Don't you want to look at it?"

"I'm not sure," he told her honestly.

"It's what you hired me for. To find out more about you."

"No, I hired you to find my brother."

She hesitated only a moment, then said quietly, "Interesting distinction. Didn't it ever occur to you that finding out about your brother would wind up making you find out more about yourself, too? You're twins, after all."

He sighed heavily, sipped his drink again and strode back to the center of the room. He felt lost in his own home. And he had no idea what to do about that.

"When I hired you," he began slowly, "I hadn't really fully considered everything that would be involved in this undertaking. All I knew then was that I wanted to find my brother. No, it never occurred to me that, in the process, I would also be discovering a lot about myself. And now I'm not sure they're things I really want to know."

Roxy wandered back toward him, shifting the file folder to her other hand. "I guess that's understandable."

He wondered if she really could understand. He doubted it. After all, how could Roxy understand all that when he didn't quite understand it himself?

Feeling restless, he moved to the sofa and took a seat, then inclined his head to the opposite side. "Sit down, Roxy."

Her eyes narrowed some at his command, but he was too tired and preoccupied to be bothered by any irritation she might feel at his imperiousness. When he made no move to apologize or amend his statement, she turned her back on him, strode in the opposite direction and sat down in a wing chair by the fireplace instead. A small act of rebellion, but one he duly noted. Roxy wanted him to know she wasn't one to be pushed around or told what to do. Why was he surprised by her action?

"Now tell me what you've found out," he said.

She eyed him narrowly as she slowly unlooped her scarf from around her neck. Then she opened the file folder onto her lap and began to shuffle carefully through the documents inside, as if she had all the time in the world. "You sure you want to know?" she asked.

He nodded wearily. "Yes. I'm sure."

She bowed her head in acknowledgment. "Okay. Then the first thing you should know is that your birth parents are dead."

Spencer inhaled deeply and expelled a shaky breath, feeling a tight coil of heat unwind in his midsection.

"They were killed in a car accident within a few miles of your house in Richmond. Evidently, you—and your twin— were with a sitter at the time."

He set his drink on the end table, propped his elbows on his knees and buried his hands in his hair. But he said nothing. The fact that his parents were dead shouldn't surprise him. It was what he had suspected all along, he reminded himself. So why did it hit him so profoundly? When he felt Roxy's gaze still fixed on him, he looked up to eye her levelly, silently indicating his wish that she be straight with him, but fearing nonetheless what she would tell him.

Before he could say a word, however, she informed him, "The second thing you should know is that I found your twin. At least, I found your twin's original birth certificate, and that's all I need to start searching."

His heart began to trip-hammer wildly. What Roxy was about to tell him was information he had craved since he was a child. A curiosity that had plagued him for as long as he could remember, that had kept him awake nights, that had prevented him from doing his work at times, was about to be assuaged. He was going to learn about that other half of him,

a man who looked just like him, but who was otherwise unfamiliar in every way. A man who had been walking the earth
for as long as Spencer had, who shared an identical genetic
makeup, but who had experiences entirely different from his
own.

His mirror image. A total stranger.

All Spencer could manage to utter was a feeble, "You
did?"

Roxy nodded.

"What…what's his name?"

She bit her lip and eyed him thoughtfully for a moment,
but didn't say anything in response.

"Roxy?" he encouraged. "What's his name?"

She dropped her gaze to the floor for a moment, and when
she looked up again, she was smiling. "His name…his name
is Charlotte."

Six

Spencer closed his eyes and rubbed them hard, then realized that gesture wasn't going to improve his hearing at all. Surely he had misunderstood.

"Charlotte?" he repeated. "My twin brother is named Charlotte?"

Her smiled grew broader. "No, your twin *sister* is named Charlotte."

He hesitated, still not sure he had heard correctly. "My...my sister?"

"Yup. Your sister."

"But...but that's impossible. I have a twin brother."

She laughed a little and shook her head. "Um, no. No, you don't. Yours was in fact a multiple birth. Fraternal twins. One boy, one girl. Stephen James and Charlotte Ellen McCormick. She's seventeen minutes older than you."

This time Spencer was the one to laugh. A nervous, anxious laugh, granted, but still the result of a ripple of delight that wound through him. "I have a big sister?" he asked with a smile.

Roxy nodded. "Congratulations. It's a girl."

She stood and moved quickly across the room, then sat right beside him on the sofa. She opened the file folder and riffled through a number of yellowed pages until she found the one she wanted.

"Once I had your birth mother's name," she began, "I was able to go back to the Bureau of Vital Statistics and check your birth date until I found a listing under her name for the other birth. It was that simple. Here's a copy of your sister's original birth certificate."

She handed the photostat copy to Spencer, who gazed down at it in much the same way he had his own a week earlier. Mother, Sherry McCormick. Father, James McCormick. Multiple birth. Richmond, Virginia. All the information was identical to his own. Except for the name, and the box marked *gender*. His twin was most definitely female, if her birth certificate was correct.

"How did you get this?" he asked.

"Fake ID," she told him. "I just made up a Virginia driver's license with my picture and Charlotte's name, then filled out an application for the birth certificate."

He stared at her, bemused. "Just how many laws are you going to have to break before this thing is done?"

She shrugged, obviously unconcerned. "As many as it takes."

He shook his head, but returned his attention to the document in his hand. "A sister," he said softly. "I had no idea."

"Of course, she won't be Charlotte Ellen McCormick anymore," Roxy told him. "She'll more than likely have the name her adopted parents gave her. She was still young enough that they probably would have changed it. Certainly, she'll have their last name, which is going to make finding her a bit difficult. It will be even tougher if she's married and has changed her name again."

Spencer glanced up, worried. "But not impossible?"

Roxy quickly shook her head. "No, not impossible. But it will take some time. I have several avenues I can investigate, and I'm still trying to decide which one would be the fastest. I'll be honest with you, Spencer. This could take a while."

Strangely, that didn't bother him. It was enough now to have a name, to have some inkling of his family history. To know he was connected to another human being out there, physically, psychologically, emotionally, spiritually.

"That's okay," he told her. "It's just nice to know I'm not alone anymore."

She smiled again and cupped her hand over the back of the one he had rested on the sofa between them. "No, you're not alone," she assured him.

He looked down at the small hand barely covering his own, then flipped his hand so that his palm brushed against hers. Then he tucked his fingers between hers and closed them snugly. "Thanks, Roxy."

She uttered a restless sound. "That's okay, Spencer. Like I said before—it's my job."

"Maybe so, but..."

She tried to tug her hand free of his, but he held on to her tight, because he just wasn't ready to let her go. When she realized that, she relaxed her hand without comment, then curled her fingers softly over the back of his hand until he could scarcely tell where her fingers ended and his began. It was a nice feeling, one he'd never quite experienced before.

With one final squeeze of his hand, she said, "I'll leave the file here. In addition to your adoption records, there's as much information as I could find about your parents, their deaths and your sister. As far as I can tell, there were no surviving relatives to take care of the two of you, which is why you became wards of the state and were ultimately put up for adoption. But you can read all that for yourself. There's not a lot in that file, but it's a start."

She began to rise from the sofa, so he pulled her back down. She landed with a softly uttered *oof* beside him, the fall throwing her off balance until she teetered over into him. He steadied her by catching her in his arms, then pulled her close. But he only gazed down at her and said nothing, mainly because he wasn't sure what he wanted to tell her.

"Spencer?" she asked when her gaze met his. Her expression indicated that she was obviously confused.

"You're not going to leave, are you?" he asked her.

She struggled to sit up, but he held her firmly in place. Finally, she surrendered and let herself be held. But there was a rigidity in her posture that he didn't like, a stiffness that told him she wasn't comfortable with the position. And not because she felt threatened by him, either. He could tell that by the look in her eyes. Her confusion mirrored his, but he didn't care. She just felt too good to let go.

"Well, yeah," she told him softly in response to his question. "I thought I would. I figure you to look over this stuff in private. If you have any questions, you can call me."

"I'd rather you stay here while I'm looking over it. That way if I have any questions, I can just ask you."

"But—"

"If you're hungry, we can send out for dinner."

As if taking the cue, her stomach rumbled noisily again, and she blushed furiously as she clutched her abdomen.

Spencer laughed. "There's a great restaurant on M Street that delivers to me all the time. They have a nice, varied menu—just about anything you could want. How about if I call and order in?"

"You don't have to do that," she told him. "I'm really not that hungry." But her stomach growled again, and this time she laughed, too.

"The way it sounds, you're not only starving, you're not going to make it down the front walk without passing out. When was the last time you ate?"

She shrugged guiltily. "I had a bowl of Frosted Flakes for breakfast."

"You haven't eaten since then?"

Roxy shook her head, but didn't elaborate. She didn't want to tell him it was because she'd spent her last two dollars on a cup of coffee and a lottery ticket. "I wasn't hungry until now," she lied.

"Then how about staying for dinner?"

His eyes were so blue, she noted, trying to tamp down an

errant sigh and forcing herself not to snuggle more eagerly against him. So blue, so earnest, so beautiful...so lost. He wasn't the kind of man who would ever beg for anything. Yet with that one look, he seemed more needful and desperate than any human being she'd ever met.

"Please, Roxy?" he asked further.

When she still didn't reply, he slightly curved the fingers of his free hand and stroked the backs of his knuckles softly over her cheek. Then he brushed his fingertips lightly over her mouth before skimming them down along her neck. He paused at the indentation at the base of her throat, tracing an idle circle there with his thumb. Then he covered her pulse with the tip of his finger and smiled when he realized how rapidly her heart was pumping.

"Don't go," he said softly. "Stay here with me. Just for a little while. Just until I have a chance to sort all this out."

Her skin was hot everywhere he touched her, and growing warmer by the second. And his eyes... It just wasn't fair that a man had such beautiful eyes.

"I... Okay."

She should be ashamed of herself, she thought, embarrassed by the immediacy of the way she caved in. Show a little backbone, for criminy's sake, she commanded herself. At least make him promise to buy dessert, too.

But she said nothing. She only sat there on the sofa, willing him to hold her even closer, at the same time terrified of what would happen when he did. Thankfully, he dropped his fingers back to his side and released her, then stood and moved away from the couch. Vaguely, she heard him pick up the telephone and dial, sort of listened while he spoke to someone on the other end of the line, then held her breath until he returned to her side.

"I'll just go make sure we have some wine to go with it," he said as he left the room instead.

And Roxy didn't think she'd ever been more grateful for such a boring statement.

Spencer's idea of "ordering in" was a whole lot different from Roxy's. When she had food delivered to her place, some long-haired teenager with a surly attitude from Pizza Dan's would show up at her door with a large deep-dish garbage special—one she would then hastily consume on the couch in her office while listening to "Car Talk" on NPR. For Spencer, however, two white-jacketed, black-bow-tied, impeccably groomed waiters arrived at his front door, each carrying dish after dish covered with a stainless-steel dome. After brief, formal greetings for Spencer, they made their way quickly to the dining room, where they tossed a crisp white linen over the table before setting it with restaurant-issue, white bone china.

Roxy watched with amazement as the two young men lit candles, arranged fresh flowers in a vase at the table's center, then retreated to the kitchen, where they proceeded to make all kinds of noise indicating they knew the procedure—and the house—very well. A moment later, one returned brandishing a silver tray that contained two glasses of pale yellow wine.

"I hope you don't mind," Spencer said absently as he took one glass and handed it to Roxy, then lifted the other for himself. He nodded his thanks to the waiter, who then disappeared back to the kitchen without a word. "But since you weren't familiar with the menu, I went ahead and ordered for us both."

Roxy was still too dumbfounded to speak, so she simply sipped her wine and nodded.

He had lifted his own glass to his lips, but stopped short of tasting it when he saw her reaction. "You do mind?" he asked.

She rolled the mildly flavored wine around in her mouth, marveling at the difference between it and the screw-off-cap kind that she normally bought at the supermarket. Spencer's selection was so much better that she wanted to savor it, so instead of swallowing, she simply shook her head this time in response to his question.

He sighed his exasperation. "Well, which is it? Yes or no? I hope I didn't offend you."

"No," she said when she finally swallowed her wine. "You didn't offend me. I don't mind."

And oddly enough, she didn't. Normally, she would consider a man rude for not asking her what she wanted for dinner. In Spencer's case, however, the gesture seemed old-fashioned and gentlemanly.

"It's nothing fancy," he added, "just chicken, salad, that kind of thing, but they do it beautifully at this place."

Nothing fancy, Roxy repeated to herself. Right. If this was his idea of nothing fancy, she couldn't imagine what he would consider formal.

Once again the starkness of their life-style differences struck her, and she wondered what it must have been like for him growing up the way he had. She couldn't imagine a life of such privilege and luxury. Nor was she sure she would want to live this way, even if the opportunity presented itself. It seemed like an awful lot of trouble.

She wondered if Spencer realized how close he had come to knowing none of this. Had he grown up as Steve McCormick instead, with parents who were blue-collar, middle class, he might be a lot more like her—struggling to make ends meet, living from paycheck to paycheck, putting off buying the things he wanted, even the things he needed.

Had Spencer's birth parents lived, had he grown up in middle-class America instead of high society, had his entire value system been based on needing instead of having, he and Roxy would probably have a lot in common. And whatever this odd heat was burning up the air between them, it might have a chance to grow. As it was, however, she could see little potential in any romantic entanglement that might involve the two of them. Maybe opposites attracted, but did they ever do anything productive once they were together?

Was destiny prevailing where she and Spencer were concerned? Or was it being overrun?

She supposed neither of them would ever find out. There simply was no way to know what Spencer's life would have been like if his birth parents had lived. Yes, in being adopted, he'd grown up with loving parents and everything money could buy. But his birth parents had doubtless been every bit as loving. And even if they wouldn't have been able to provide him with the education and luxuries he had received, Spencer—or rather, Steve—would probably have been perfectly content with his life, both past and present.

For some reason, Roxy wasn't sure that was true of Spencer. Although he gave no indication that he was *un*happy, he didn't seem particularly *happy,* either. There seemed to be something missing in him, but she couldn't quite put her finger on what. She hoped that in helping him find his sister, Roxy could help Spencer find that missing part of himself, too.

But that's not what he's paying you for, she reminded herself. *That missing part stuff is none of your business. You do missing persons, not missing pieces, remember?*

Even though Roxy told herself that, she knew there was no way she'd ever believe it. Missing pieces were as much a part of her life as oxygen was. Searching, seeking…those were the things she did. It was the finding part she had trouble with, at least where her own life was concerned. Maybe her desire to help Spencer was generated by the fact that she hadn't been able to help herself. Maybe she wanted to see him become whole because she knew she never would be herself.

Whatever.

Speculation is for suckers, she told herself, pushing the thoughts away. *Just do your damned job and get it over with.*

And then Roxy knew she could go back to living her life the way it was supposed to be lived. On her own. All alone.

For all its strangeness, dinner wound up being a comfortable, uneventful repast. Once it was over, the two waiters cleaned up, packed up and disappeared, and Spencer and Roxy returned to the living room with the last of the wine filling their glasses.

Spencer went immediately to the sofa and scooped up the manila folder that held his adoption record, still not certain he was ready to plumb further into what Roxy had discovered.

But he had started this thing, he reminded himself, and in spite of the fact that he'd been ill-prepared for the snowballing repercussions that had ensued, he had no choice but to see it through to its end.

So, wordlessly, he took the folder to a desk in the corner, sat down behind it, flicked on a lamp, donned a pair of reading glasses, loosened his tie and opened the file. The last time he looked at Roxy, she was sitting on the sofa, thumbing through the latest issue of *Architectural Digest.*

When he looked up again, two hours had passed in silence, Spencer was more confused than he'd ever been in his life and Roxy was curled up on the sofa, sound asleep, hiking boots neglected on the floor.

For one dizzying moment, he completely forgot who he was. Where he was. What he was supposed to be doing. For the past two hours, he had been utterly immersed in the short life of Stephen James McCormick and the tragic deaths of the young boy's parents. He'd gone through the entire adoption process, from the reclamation of Stephen by the state of Virginia, to the orphanage where he had spent the next four weeks, to the interview and background check of the two people he had known all his life as his parents, and ultimately to the house where he grew up.

A social worker had called at that house on a regular basis in those early months, to make sure the new family was settling in nicely. But Spencer could remember none of that. All he could remember was two people who had loved him very much, who had celebrated his birthday every year with a huge party, who had made sure every Christmas was one to remember. Two people who had given him a life he would never have known otherwise.

Stephen James McCormick had become Spencer Mason Melbourne. There was no Steve. There was only Spencer. The two men were one and the same.

Spencer took off his reading glasses and tossed them onto the desk. Then he rubbed his eyes with the heels of his palms and sighed heavily. What the hell was he doing? he wondered. Trying to chart the life of a man who never lived. Stephen

James McCormick was no more real than the tooth fairy was. Yet Spencer just couldn't shake his curiosity—his hunger for knowledge—about the man.

With his eyes still covered by his hands, he asked himself the question he had been asking himself all week. Where would he be right this minute if he hadn't been adopted? If his birth parents had just left their house two minutes later and never been hit head-on by that furniture delivery truck?

Would he be working that middle-management position at the auto factory as Roxy had suggested? Would his closet be filled with clothes from JC Penney instead of Barney's? Would he drive a Dodge Caravan instead of a Porsche 911 Cabriolet? Would he spend hours trying to figure out how the hell he was going to make the mortgage payment now that his daughter needed braces and his son wanted to take clarinet lessons, instead of buying whatever he wanted, whenever he wanted it? And would there be a woman in the picture some-where, someone to cling to every night when he felt like the demands of his life were sucking him dry?

Steve might have problems that would never plague Spen-cer. But he might have other things, too, that Spencer would never have. And when he got right down to it, which life was the better one, really?

Spencer dropped his hands onto his desk in loose fists. There was no way he would ever know, and it was pointless for him to expend so much energy worrying about what might have been. But he knew no matter how often and fiercely he told himself that, he still might never shake his confusion where his identity was concerned.

Involuntarily, his gaze traveled toward the sofa, lingering on Roxy as she slept so blissfully unaware of his own turmoil. From the moment he had met her, he'd been impressed with the fact that she seemed so sure of herself. In spite of the clear fact that she was struggling by a thread in many areas of her life, she made no excuses or explanations for who she was. He envied her that—her confidence in and certainty of herself that threatened to overwhelm him at times. She was simply Roxanne Matheny, take her or leave her.

Spencer wanted to take her. But what would he do with her once he had her?

Without really thinking about his intentions, he pushed his chair away from the desk with a soft scrape. Roxy uttered a quiet sigh at the hushed sound, but remained otherwise motionless. She must be exhausted, he thought, to be sleeping so deeply so early in the evening. He hoped she hadn't overextended herself in this particular case. Then he immediately countered that thought by hoping she would give it every bit of her attention. Not just because he was so eager to find his twin sister, but because he suddenly wanted Roxy's life to be as fully enmeshed with his as it could possibly be.

He stood silently and made his way as quietly as he could across the room. Even when he crouched down on the floor beside her head, she never moved. He lifted a hand and ran his fingertip lightly over her cheek, marveling at the softness and warmth of her skin. She exhaled a soft sound and turned a bit, but still she didn't awaken.

Spencer smiled. He should probably rouse her and take her home. But something prevented him from doing so. He told himself it was only because he didn't have the heart to wake her up, and not because it just felt so good—so much less lonely—to have someone else in the house. He stood and reached for the heavy cotton throw that was folded neatly on the back of the couch, shook it open and draped it over Roxy's lower half. Then he returned to his desk, snapped off the light and stood for a moment in the darkness.

Maybe Steve McCormick would indeed have a woman waiting for him when he came home from work every night, Spencer thought. But that woman wouldn't be Roxanne Matheny.

He made his way to the stairway in the foyer and climbed the carpeted steps slowly. Only once did he turn around, to see Roxy still sleeping soundly in a pale rectangle of light that spilled through the window. He smiled. And suddenly, for some reason, Spencer wasn't so sure that Steve would be the happier man, after all.

Seven

Roxy awoke in the same surroundings she always awoke in. She was on the couch, and the room was dark, except for a hint of yellowish light cascading through the window from a street lamp outside. But where the neighborhood around her office was generally noisy and wide-awake in the wee hours of the morning, this time she had awakened to silence.

Only then did she realize that the light from the street lamp outside was filtering through a crystal clear, six-over-six window, and not the grimy glass behind her desk. The couch she slept on was an overstuffed fabric one that was *very* comfortable, and not the squeaky yellow Naugahyde one in her outer office whose duct tape patches scratched her thighs.

Then she remembered that she was in Spencer's house. The last thing she recalled was watching him as he pored over the contents of his adoption file, noting the way his fingers twisted anxiously in his hair, marveling that he looked even better with his reading glasses on than he had without them. She recalled how the wine had made her sleepy, and how she'd stretched out on the sofa for just a minute—just long enough to rest her eyes. Evidently her eyes had been a lot more tired than she'd realized.

She angled her wrist toward the window, squinting at her watch in the faint light. Jeez, almost two-fifteen. It was going to be murder trying to get home this time of night. She always tried to be safely locked inside by midnight, because that was when the streets below her office starting revving to life. That was when the hookers and the junkies crawled out of their cribs to look for a little easy action, when the pimps and the pushers sponsored happy hour. That's when folks like Roxy were better off tucked in bed with the covers up over their heads.

This time of night, she'd be lucky to make it back with her wallet—and her virtue—intact. Not that her wallet was particularly fat with gold or her virtue particularly sterling. But a woman couldn't be too careful when she was living among riffraff.

She rubbed her eyes and stretched, and noted for the first time the cotton throw that had become tangled around her legs. She smiled. Obviously, Spencer didn't mind her staying the night, she thought. He could have awakened her and sent her on her merry way hours ago. For a moment, she wondered why he hadn't, then decided quickly that it was because of the inherent decency that seemed to be so deeply ingrained in him. Nevertheless, Roxy Matheny wasn't the kind of woman who took advantage of a person's hospitality. Especially when the person in question was upstairs sleeping, maybe even in the buff, and it would be just too, too easy to go up there and—

She halted the thought before it had a chance to gel in her brain. No sense making herself crazy.

Her stomach rumbled as it had earlier that evening, and she figured Spencer wouldn't mind if she grabbed a couple of those brown rolls left over from their dinner for the road. She found her way to the kitchen, padded quietly across to the oversize refrigerator, then mumbled irritably at the bright, white light that tumbled from inside when she opened the door. She was wrapping two of the hard rolls in a paper towel when the brighter, whiter light overhead snapped on, something that made her curse out loud as she spun quickly around.

Spencer stood in the doorway, one hand on the light switch, the other settled casually on his hip. He was barefoot, his dark blue, silk pajama bottoms knotted loosely at his waist, a matching robe gaping open over his naked chest. Roxy bit her lip. She had wondered about that chest—a lot—ever since bumping into it a week ago. And she'd had no idea that reality could be so much more vivid than her fantasies.

Dark hair scattered across the top from shoulder to shoulder, narrowing gradually to a thin line at his flat belly that lured her gaze to follow it to where it disappeared beneath the waistband of his pajamas. His abdominal muscles were truly things of beauty, each lovingly defined beneath taut swells of flesh. If she had a mind to, she could walk right over and trace her fingertips along the sturdy lines of each one, and she wasn't much surprised to discover that she did indeed have a mind to do just that.

But instead of acting on her impulse, her fingers curled convulsively over the rolls she still clutched in her hands, nearly mashing them into ineffective little balls of dough.

"Um, gee, you caught me stealing bread on my way out," she said sheepishly, hoping the shakiness of her heart rate wasn't reflected in her voice. "Used to be, you could get a life of hard labor or shipped off to Australia for that. What's the penalty nowadays?"

Even though she hadn't yet mustered the courage to look at his face, Roxy was somehow certain that the penalties he was conjuring in his head were far more reaching than simple incarceration. For some reason, handcuffs came to mind. And blindfolds. And…feathers?

But all he said was, "On your way out? Just where do you think you're going at this hour?"

"I, um…" She eyed his chest again, then finally managed to force her gaze above his neck. And she saw that he was smiling. "I have to get home," she said lamely.

His smile fell. "Is there someone there worrying about you?"

"No," she said without thinking. "I mean…" Damn, she thought. If she had just said yes, she might have been able to preserve the distance between them that she felt shrinking more and more with each passing minute.

His smile returned. "If there's no one waiting for you at home, then what's the rush? It's the middle of the night, for God's sake. Stay until morning. Have some breakfast."

She held up the rolls. "What do you think these are going to be?"

He moved silently across the kitchen floor, pausing several inches before her. In her stocking feet, Roxy stood a good foot shorter than he, and she found herself staring at his chest. Again. He smelled wonderful, though, as if he had showered just before he went to bed, soaping up with something clean and spicy and utterly masculine. She lifted her gaze just a fraction, noting that his jaws were covered with a healthy growth of rough beard, and she remembered the way his face had abraded hers the week before when he kissed her. She tried to chase the image away, but it remained fixed firmly at the forefront of her brain.

Evidently oblivious to her dilemma, he asked, "You're actually *stealing* your breakfast?"

Inhaling a deep breath, she replied, "Well, no, not stealing, actually. More like, um…"

"Like what?"

She sighed fitfully. "Okay, stealing. But when you steal from a friend, it's not a crime."

He studied her thoughtfully for a moment. "You consider me to be a friend?"

Major understatement, Roxy thought. But all she said was, "Sure."

"Then stay the night."

"Oh, I don't think—"

"What's wrong, Roxy? Are you worried about what might happen between the two of us?"

"Of course not," she lied. "Why would you even ask a question like that?"

He shrugged, but there was nothing casual about the gesture. "Maybe because *I'm* worried about what might happen between the two of us."

She didn't—couldn't—say anything. All she could do was tilt her head back more and look into his eyes, and watch fascinated as the fire she saw burning there grew hotter and brighter.

"The reason I came down here just now," he began again, "is because I've been lying in bed for the past two hours, wide-awake, trying to come up with an excuse to wake you up, too."

Still, she was unable to respond. She knew she *should* respond, knew she should say something to stop him, but for the life of her, she couldn't think of a thing. Much to her irritation, she realized she actually wanted him to go on, wanted to hear what he had to say, wanted to see if he'd been wondering about the same things that she'd been wondering about lately. She wanted to find out if he'd been thinking of making love to her the way she'd been thinking of making love to him. So instead of stopping him, she met his gaze levelly and silently encouraged him to continue.

And he did. "Once you were awake," he said softly, lifting a hand to her hair and curling a few idle strands around his fingers, "I was trying to come up with an excuse to get close to you."

Roxy wet her lips and swallowed hard. But still she said nothing.

"And then," he continued, taking a step toward her, "once I was close to you, I was trying to come up with an excuse to…"

His voice trailed off, but she was certain it wasn't because he didn't know what he was going to say. His tone was just too devilish for her to doubt that he had something specific in mind.

"To what?" she finally managed to whisper.

"To get you naked."

"Oh, no."

"To get you into my bed."

"Oh, Spencer."

"To make love to you."

"Oh, boy."

She could see in his eyes that he was perfectly intent on making good on his plan, and she told herself she should be shocked by his suggestion. Truth was, however, that she was more than a little curious herself to see what kind of sparks would fly between them. Still, she reminded herself, that was no reason to play the sap.

"I have to go," she said again.

"Roxy…"

"No, Spencer, I mean it. I have to go."

She dropped the rolls she'd been mangling during their exchange onto the counter and reached for her scarf. Spencer grabbed the other end, though, and yanked it hard. Roxy made a halfhearted effort to pull it back, but within seconds, she wound up letting herself be tugged toward him.

"Don't go," he said again.

"I have to."

"Why?"

"Because it's pointless to encourage this attraction we have for each other."

"Why?"

"Because there's no future in it."

"Why?"

"Because…"

He tugged on the scarf again, bringing her body flush against his. "Why, Roxy?"

She knew why. Because she had been down this road before. Because once upon a time, a long, long time ago, a rich boy with black hair and blue eyes had promised her everything and left her with nothing. Because Spencer was the same kind of man that boy would have grown up to be. He and Roxy were too different, came from two entirely opposite backgrounds. The first time their relationship was put to the social and cultural test, she'd wind up being shoved out the back door. Just like she had been before. She knew it. Down in the deepest, darkest part of her heart, she knew exactly how Spencer Melbourne would treat her once he got tired of sampling her way of life.

Yet she told him none of this. Instead, she just whispered, "Because…because this is crazy, that's why."

"No," he said with a shake of his head. "This isn't crazy. You want to know what will make it crazy?"

She didn't reply, only continued to lose herself in the deep blue depths of his eyes.

He looped the scarf around her shoulders, and with one final yank, he hauled her up against him. "*This* is crazy."

Before she had a chance to respond, he covered her mouth with his, tracing the outline of her lips with his tongue before sucking the lower one inside to taste it more fully. The tip of his tongue skimmed lightly over her lip, and Roxy felt herself beginning a slow downward spiral to a warm and exotic place. Her reservations of only moments ago evaporated like so much steam, and all she could do was sink against him, helpless to resist whatever he had in store. As if of their own free will, her hands wandered up along his hips and waist, her fingers curling into the cool, soft fabric of his robe.

She'd never felt this kind of silk before, and was surprised at how quickly it warmed beneath her touch, much as Spencer's skin did when she moved her hand to his chest. The dark coils of hair wound easily around her fingers, as if trying to imprison them against his chest. Roxy splayed her hand open wide over his heart, felt its steady *thump-thump-thump* become not so steady, then inched her fingers up to his neck, covering his pulse with her thumb. Again, she marveled at his irregular heartbeat, amazed that she could be the cause of it.

So caught up had she become in exploring him that she was surprised when she felt his hand suddenly slide down to cradle her buttocks. He pressed his fingers into her soft flesh, then rubbed erratic, erotic circles over her fanny. His gesture served to bring her pelvis forward, and she felt him swell to life against her belly. A groan erupted from a dark and empty place deep inside her, and he silenced the voice of her desire by covering her mouth with his again, driving his tongue as deeply into her as he could.

He dipped a hand beneath her sweater, then dragged the fabric up along her body until his fingers found one lace-covered breast. Immediately, he covered the warm mound entirely with his hand, palming the peak to rigid delight. Roxy's exhaled breath was a mixture of sigh and gasp, but she lifted her own hand over the part of her sweater that hid his. Through the heavy fabric, she clutched his hand in hers, steering it to her other breast, encouraging the same languid circles there.

Spencer allowed her to guide him lower then, obeying her eagerly when she directed his hand down over her flat belly and in between her legs. Only then did she release him, not because she wanted him to stop, but because she needed to cling to him with both hands when the explosion of sensation he wreaked in her nearly undid her. He rubbed his fingers against the damp cloth of her leggings, and Roxy felt her legs grow weak. When they finally buckled under her completely, Spencer caught her ably, spreading wide his fingers at that warm apex, hauling her up against him.

He fondled her all the way through the living room and up the stairs to his bedroom, stopping only when he lowered her to the bed, and only long enough to shrug out of his robe and pajama bottoms. Then he stood before her naked, the watery moonlight spilling in long stripes through the open blinds, gilding every hard plane of his body with silver.

"You're right," she finally managed to say. "This is crazy. We shouldn't be doing this."

But instead of meeting his eye when she spoke, her gaze lingered elsewhere, on a part of him that had preoccupied her for some time. He was, in a word, magnificent. Large and hard and quite clearly ready to bury himself deep inside her waiting warmth. And in spite of the fact that she had just assured him that she considered what was happening between them to be a mistake, she lowered her hands to the hem of her sweater and pulled it slowly, leisurely, over her head.

"Wait," he said when she reached for the back closure of her brassiere. "Let me."

He joined her on the bed, kneeling before her, but instead of moving his hands behind her to unhook her bra, he cupped her face in his palms. "You are so beautiful, Roxy," he whispered reverently. "Not just in body, but in spirit. In soul. You're so..." He paused, seeming at a loss for words. Finally, he concluded, "I've just never met a woman like you before."

She tried to brush off the knot that clenched tight in her belly at his roughly uttered declaration. She tried to remind herself that what he had just told her was the problem—she was a novelty, nothing more. She tried to convince herself that the only reason he was with her now was because he wanted a taste of something different—something less refined, less inhibited, less governed by polite society. She told herself he pictured her as someone easy, someone wild, someone likely to indulge in things his more conventional lovers would never try.

Unfortunately, she couldn't convince herself that he was such a man at all. Unfortunately, all she could see was someone who was as wanting and lonely as she was herself, and all she could do was respond to him in a way that defied everything she knew to be reasonable and safe. She could no more resist Spencer than she could resist the breath that gave her life. She needed him. It was that simple. There was no way she could turn back now.

In spite of that, she tried to be flip as she countered, "You're not likely to meet too many more women like me in the future, either, if you're lucky." But the cool distance of the statement was completely at odds with the feelings that raged rampant in her heart.

He smiled and brushed his thumbs lightly over both her cheeks. "I think I'm very lucky. So it shouldn't be necessary to meet any more women—like you or not—in the future."

She opened her mouth to say something, anything, that would ease some of the import inherent in his words, but

Spencer stopped her by placing his hand lightly over her mouth.

"Don't," he said simply. "Don't say anything more." Then he dropped his hands to her shoulders and instructed her, "Turn around."

She did as he requested, slowly pivoting on her knees, shoving aside the rumpled bedclothes as she did so. Spencer's warm fingertips dipped beneath the band of her bra, deftly loosing the two hooks that bound it together. Immediately, the wisp of lace fell off her shoulders, and he helped it along, skimming it down her arms before discarding it in a puff of white onto the floor. Then she felt him move behind her, pressing his chest to her naked back, and she leaned into him as he moved his hands to her front and covered her breasts.

He rolled her nipples between his thumbs and forefingers, then squeezed them gently. Roxy's eyelids fluttered down over her eyes, and she reached behind herself, over her shoulders, to bury her fingers in his hair. His rigid shaft pressed taut against her back, and she grew warm and damp in response. He continued to pump one breast, but dipped his other hand lower, down along her flat belly, to the waistband of her leggings.

"Let's get rid of these," he said softly from behind her.

She nodded, not certain she could trust her voice at this point, and let him peel the tight fabric down over her thighs along with her panties. She shifted enough to let him remove the garments completely, then he pulled her back, and she leaned against him again, fully naked and fully aroused.

"That's better," he whispered, his mouth hovering right above her ear.

He moved his hands to her breasts again, and she reached behind her to spread her palms open over his hips. His skin was hot beneath her touch, taut and steely hard. Again she felt his hard shaft pressing against her lower back, and without even planning to, she moved one hand to circle its base.

She heard him gasp, then growl, then he ducked his head to the curve where her shoulder met her neck. He shoved her hair aside and pressed a kiss to her nape, followed by another, then another, then another. With every brush of his lips against her neck, Roxy stroked her palm along the length of him. And every time she stroked her palm against him, she felt him leap to life, felt him grow stiffer and fuller in her hand.

And then he suddenly pulled away from her completely, curving his hands over her shoulders to turn her around to face him. Her puzzlement must have shown on her face, because he smiled softly and said, "I want to make this last as long as possible. The way we were going, that wasn't likely to be the case."

"Spencer, I—"

"Shh…" he whispered, placing a finger gently over her lips. "No more talking. Let's just let this happen. Let's just feel what's going on between us."

"But—"

"Shh…"

Roxy obeyed him, simply because she didn't have the strength to protest any further. She cupped her hands behind his neck, pulled his head down to hers and kissed him. Long and hard and deep. He bent forward and anchored his hands on the mattress—one on each side of her—and slowly urged her backward onto the bed. The sheet beneath her bare back was cool, but the man lying atop her was warm. He nestled between her legs, buried his hands in her hair and held her head steady while he plundered her mouth with his.

After taking his fill from her there, he moved his head lower, to her breasts. He suckled first one and then the other, flattening his tongue against her warm flesh, tasting the undersides and peaks, circling each nipple before taking as much of each mound as he could into his mouth, pulling and pulling and pulling until she thought she would go mad.

When he quenched his thirst there, he moved lower, dipping his tongue into her navel for a brief taste before sipping her skin down to the soft dark curls that offered little protection from his plunder. His hands settled briefly between her thighs, but only long enough to spread her legs apart and win better access to the treasure he sought. For a few dizzying moments, he investigated the heated core of her with curious fingers, then thumbed her open and followed his exploration with an equally avid mouth.

Roxy had never experienced such an intimate, arousing gesture. At first, she was unable to move, so stunned was she by the sensations spiraling through her with a speed and intensity that would eclipse a supernova. All she could do was lie still, her hands twisted in the fabric of the pillowcase on each side of her head, wondering how any human being could enjoy such ecstasy without being completely done in.

Time began to dissolve into nothing, and everything around her seemed to disappear. She closed her eyes and saw a kaleidoscope of color bursting into flame, felt a hot, tight knot begin to slowly unravel in her belly. Slowly, so slowly she thought she would die, a shudder began to wind through her. It started where Spencer's tongue flicked like the kiss of a hummingbird, then steadily spread outward in spirals of heat. And then, out of nowhere, the shudder exploded, rocking her forward, bucking her hips.

Immediately, Spencer rose above her, absorbing her cries of completion into his mouth, stilling the motion of her body by covering it heavily with his. She wasn't sure how much time passed before she opened her eyes. Perhaps seconds, perhaps years. When Roxy managed to focus again, she saw Spencer propped beside her on one elbow, his hand cupping her breast, his thumb tracing idle circles on the warm flesh.

"Are you all right?" he asked, smiling.

She managed to nod wearily. "I think so."

His smile grew broader. "Good. Because we still have a lot of ground to cover."

Her focus began to grow hazy. "We do?"

He chuckled low, and she didn't think she'd ever heard a more arousing sound in her life. "Oh, yeah."

She sighed heavily, somehow finding the strength to circle her arms behind his neck. "Then by all means...lead on."

She had thought about asking him where he was going to take her, but she figured out quickly that they were on the road to stark, utter delight when he leaned over her and reached for something in the nightstand drawer. She knew the precaution was necessary, knew he was thinking of her safety and well-being as much as he was his own. But even this small invasion of reality reminded Roxy that what she was doing was going to come back to haunt her. It wasn't quite the fantasy it seemed.

Then she ceased to think at all, because Spencer traced his fingers slowly down her neck and along the slick skin between her breasts. His fingers hovered over the part of her he had just driven to a frenzy, then he levered his body over hers.

"But you haven't—" she began.

"Shh…"

"But I didn't—"

"Shh… This is for you, Roxy, not me."

She chuckled, a fragile, feeble sound. "Oh, yeah?"

He chuckled in response. "Okay, it's for me, too. But later. Right now, I want to be inside you."

She wanted to tell him he was already inside her. That he'd been inside her since the day he'd walked into her office looking so confused and lost. But before she could say a word, he entered her, and the words—along with her breath— caught in her throat.

He seemed to fuse into her. His flesh, so hard and taut and hot, seemed to become one with her own. Roxy could scarcely tell where Spencer ended and she began, wondered if the two of them would ever be able to separate again. Then he moved, pulled himself out of her again and drove himself in more deeply, more resolutely. Roxy gasped at the depth he seemed to reach, knowing he'd touched her in a way no man had touched her before, searing himself indelibly inside her, no matter what happened afterward, when they parted.

He was inside her. Just as he'd wanted to be. Just as she knew he would be forever.

Eight

Spencer awoke to faint darkness, his chest sheened with perspiration, his heart pounding, his breathing shallow and scanty. He'd had a dream. Not *the* dream, but one every bit as realistic and disturbing, and one that left him with the certain knowledge of someone else like him in the world. Only this time, that someone else like him was hurting. This time, his twin was in danger. This time, his sister's very life was on the line. He didn't know how he knew that—he just *knew*. Charlotte was in trouble. He had to find her fast.

He'd been alone in the dream this time, scared out of his wits. Flames had licked at him, and he'd been seared by a heat like none he could ever have imagined. He hadn't been able to breathe, hadn't been able to see. All around him had been blackness and heat—he'd been able to taste it, smell it; it had seeped into his pores and scorched his lungs and caused his skin to tingle. He had been looking for something...no, some*one*. Someone he loved, someone whose existence meant the very world to him. His fear had not been for his own life, but for that of someone else he loved.

He had been clawing at the blackness, scratching at the heat, when a loud crash had awakened him. At first, he'd thought the crash had come from inside his house, from the here and now. But since waking, he realized that the sound that had jarred him to consciousness had actually been part of his dream.

He knew this because Roxy slept peacefully on her side next to him, one arm draped across his chest, the other curled beneath her pillow. In the gray, early-morning light that turned their entwined bodies to silver, he could see the lower curve of one breast beneath her upper arm. The pin-striped sheet dipped low on her waist, just hinting at the lush curve of her hip. He felt her leg crossed over his at the thigh, and the warmth of her flesh pressing against his stirred him to life.

He exhaled sharply and raked a hand through his damp hair. God, not again. Roxy made him hungry in a way he'd never felt before. He'd made love to her twice, slamming himself deep into her with a quick, forceful penetration that was in no way like him. He felt like an animal when he was with her, his passion overriding any coherent sense of reason. There was so much desire, so much wanting, so much *need*. He'd brought her to climax nearly a half dozen times, and had tumbled over the precipice himself more than once.

And now his body was telling him it wanted another go.

He shifted his position until he, too, was lying on his side, his groin cradled against Roxy's pelvis, his hardening shaft pressing into her softness before nestling between her thighs. She made a contented sound in her sleep and snuggled closer, and he looped his arm around her waist to hold her there. She felt good in his arms, felt right in his bed. Hell, he thought further, she felt right in his life. For a moment, he let himself spin an idle fantasy of how good it could be with him and Roxy.

Then, unable to stop the memory from coming, he thought about the dream.

He glanced at the clock on the nightstand to find its glowing green numbers approaching the hour of five. The sun would be rising soon. When it did, he wondered, would his sister also be watching the faint rays of light staining the sky with hints of pink and yellow? Or would she be trapped in blackness, suffocating in heat, struggling to find her way out of the darkness that was closing in?

Wherever she was, Charlotte, or whatever her name was now, was in trouble. And Spencer had never felt so helpless in his life.

He turned to look at Roxy and was tempted to nudge her gently awake. But she felt too good beside him, felt so warm and soft and right. There would be time later in the morning to tell her about his dream. Time to talk about a lot of things the two of them needed to address.

As he closed his eyes again, his thoughts returned to his dream. And he promised himself there was still time to find his sister, too.

He awoke again to find Roxy dressing. Spencer propped himself up in bed on one elbow, scrubbed a hand over his face and didn't say a word. The light coming through the window had turned pink by now, and he watched Roxy as she tugged her bright red sweater over her head and ran both hands briskly through her hair to tame it. Obviously unaware of his observation, she paused briefly, then dropped her loosely fisted hands over her eyes. For a long moment, she didn't move, then he heard a soft sniffle, watched her rub her eyes fiercely and saw her arms fall back to her sides.

"Good morning," he said softly.

She spun quickly toward him, and even in the scant light available he could see that she looked panicked. Why, he couldn't imagine. After a night like the one they'd just spent together, he would think she would be feeling the same way he was feeling right now—relaxed and peaceful and utterly without care.

"You caught me trying to make my break again," she said, her voice a little rusty, though whether a result of the early hour or something else, Spencer wasn't sure.

"What are you planning to take with you this time?" he asked, smiling. "Other than my heart, I mean."

She returned his smile hastily, her expression anxious. "Nothing, I promise. I'll stop by the bagel place near my office on my way home."

"I'll take you home," he told her. But he made no move to rise from the bed. "Later." He patted the empty sheet next to himself, noting that the warmth and musky fragrance of her body still clung to the fabric. "Why don't you come back to bed for a little while? It's still early. Neither one of us has to be anywhere for a while."

She shook her head. "No, actually, it's very late."

When she didn't elaborate, Spencer started to ask her to clarify just what she meant by her remark. But before he had a chance, she was hustling toward the bedroom door and he realized she really was on her way out. Out of his bed, out of his room, out of his house...hell, out of his life. He jack-knifed up in bed, threw back the sheet and, still naked, raced after her.

"Where are you going?" he demanded as he followed her.

"My boots are downstairs," she called over her shoulder, neither slowing down, nor looking back.

"Roxy," he said, catching up with her at the top of the stairs. He snagged her wrist quite capably in one hand and spun her around to face him. "What's the rush?"

He could tell she wanted to stay. Badly. He could see it in her eyes. But she said nothing, moved neither toward nor away from him.

"Roxy?" he asked again.

Still she said nothing.

When he tugged on her arm to pull her back to him, she went limp. That was the only way he could describe what happened to her. Her head fell forward, her shoulders sagged, her posture slumped. Even her knees seemed to bend in defeat. But still she remained silent.

"Come back to bed," he said softly.

Finally, she shook her head, slowly, as if forcing herself to complete the action. Her mouth formed the word *no,* but the word itself never emerged.

"Why not?"

She sighed heavily, a wistful sound, then tried halfheartedly to twist her wrist free of his grasp. But Spencer continued to hold on to her, unwilling to let her go just yet.

"Spencer, please," she finally said. "Let me go. I have to get home."

"Not until we've straightened a few things out."

"There's nothing to straighten out."

"Oh, I think there's plenty to straighten out."

Her head dropped toward her chest again, and she expelled an impatient sound. "All right," she acceded. "But for God's sake, put some clothes on first. I'll meet you downstairs."

He smiled. "Why? Does the sight of me naked drive you to distraction?"

"Something like that," she replied cryptically.

"Is that such a bad thing?"

"Mmm-hmm," she muttered as her gaze skittered to some point over his shoulder. "Yeah, it's a very bad thing."

He wanted to ask her why, but figured it might be better to solve one problem before opening up another. And although he knew her comment was his cue to go put some clothes on as she'd instructed him, he still wasn't convinced he could trust her not to duck out while he was getting dressed.

Evidently, she knew exactly what he was thinking, because she added, "I won't go anywhere, I promise."

"Okay," he relented, reluctantly turning loose of her wrist. "Give me five minutes."

"I'll put some coffee on, if I can figure out how that Eurotech brewer of yours works."

She turned without looking at him and made her way down the stairs, mumbling something about whatever happened to good ol' percolated coffee, anyway, and what was the problem with buying American.

Spencer couldn't help the smile that curled his lips as he watched her go. Her hair was a mess, thanks to the advanced-class sexual gymnastics they'd engaged in the night before, a rumpled mass of dark brown that rioted atop her head like a badly orchestrated parade. But instead of being put off by the snarls and tangles, he only wanted to bury his hands even deeper in her hair and mess it up more.

He still wasn't sure what had come over him the night before. As he'd lain wide-awake in bed feeling restless and empty, he'd only known he wanted Roxy, and he'd been driven by the need to have her. Surrounded by darkness, staring up at the nothingness above him, all he'd been able to see was the two of them engaged in the most basic of couplings.

And when his fantasies had finally become too much for him to bear, he'd been compelled to seek out the source of them, only to find her trying to escape. Fortunately, once he'd discovered her, Roxy had been as eager to explore the heat that had flared up between them as he'd been, and the resulting fireworks had been more than he could ever have anticipated.

Now as he tugged on sweatpants and a white V-necked T-shirt, all he could do was want Roxy some more. He had figured that after what had occurred between them last night, this morning would be a breeze. What he hadn't counted on was that the breeze would be created by Roxy's hasty departure as she fled from him.

He padded barefoot down the stairs and found her in the living room, seated in the very extreme corner on one side of the sofa. Her boots still sat on the floor, but she had curled her body up so tightly—her knees drawn up before her, her hands tucked into opposite armpits—that she might as well have put her shoes on and left. Everything about her screamed *back off*, but Spencer was in no mood to leave her alone.

The aroma of brewing coffee roused him some, but he ignored it. Instead, he focused all of his attention on the woman seated so defensively in his house, and he couldn't help but wonder how she could feel so defensive after giving so freely of herself the night before. In spite of that, he gave her the space she silently demanded, and remained standing in the archway that separated the living room from the foyer and stairs.

"You want to tell me what's going on here?" he asked. "Why you tried to get away this morning without even saying goodbye?"

At first she didn't look at him, didn't even seem to have heard him speak. Then she moved her arms to wrap them around her knees and, without so much as glancing at him, replied, "I thought it would be easier than hanging around for a scene like this one."

"A scene like what one?"

"Like this," she said, gesturing impatiently around the room. "The dreaded morning-after scene. It's always so awkward."

"Experienced a lot of these morning-after scenes, have you?"

She picked at a nonexistent piece of lint on her sleeve. "No, of course not. But I'm no fool. I know what you're thinking."

"That's some trick. At this point, I'm not even sure *I* know what I'm thinking."

"Yeah, well, I do."

He sighed impatiently. "Care to enlighten me?"

She drew in a slow breath and expelled it in a shaky sigh. "You're thinking that you've stumbled onto a nice little diversion. That it's going to be great to have me in your bed for a while. But soon you're going to be wondering how to get rid of me."

He shook his head. "Wrong. You're not even close."

Finally, she looked at him, turned her head fully to face him and stared him right in the eye. "Oh, believe me, Spencer, I know exactly what I'm talking about here. I've taken a walk down this particular garden path before. It's old territory. If that's not what you're thinking now, it will be soon."

"Roxy—"

She cut him off by holding up one hand, palm out. "You're about to tell me that you're not going to try to get rid of me, because you really care about me, because you've never met anyone like me, because nothing like last night has ever happened to you before.''

Spencer frowned. More or less, that had indeed been pretty much what he had been about to say.

"You're going to tell me you want to see more of me, that what's happening between us is a strange and wonderful thing, and that we should see it through to its conclusion.''

Again, the wording wasn't exactly what he would have chosen, but Roxy had pegged his thoughts very well. Still, he said nothing in response, curious to hear how she thought the two of them would end up.

"Well, I can tell you what the conclusion will be. We'll have a few laughs, a little fun, then you'll gradually start to get bored. You'll start being out when I call, you'll make up excuses for why you have to leave early when you do find time to see me, and then you'll find some nice, normal, socially acceptable woman who fits your life-style a lot better than I ever will.''

She paused for a telling moment before adding, "But, of course, you won't tell that yourself. I'll find out about it when I come to your house one morning to see what the hell's happened to you, and find the new woman in your life there with you...poaching your eggs. So to speak.''

Spencer set his teeth together hard. She had this pretty well thought out. The whole thing was entirely misconceived, of course, but it was well thought out. "You know this for a fact, do you?" he asked her.

"Like I said. I've done this little number before.''

"That doesn't mean it's going to happen again.''

"Oh, yes, it does.''

"Why do you say that?''

"Because you rich guys are like that. Money does funny things to people. I'm not saying you're a bad guy, Spencer, just that you're different from me. And I'm not begrudging you your wealth, either. Hey, people ought to get what they can in this life, however they can get it. But money still does funny things to people.''

"It makes them turn their backs on people they care about, is that what you're saying?"

Her mouth tightened to a fine line. "No. Just that it...changes your perception about things. Makes you think you care about someone when, in fact, you just care about what that someone can do for you."

"And just what is it you can do for me, Roxy? In your unmonied opinion, I mean."

"I'm a slice of life you've never savored," she responded immediately. "I'm lowbrow when you're used to high. I'm peanut butter and jelly when you've gotten bored with caviar."

"That's not exactly true," he countered. "I've never much liked caviar."

She ignored his attempt at levity. "All I'm saying is that once the novelty of the social thing wears off, you'll get tired of me and dump me. And when that time comes, maybe I won't be so ready to be dumped."

Spencer frowned, wanting to contradict her. But hadn't he told himself exactly what Roxy was telling him not long ago? That making love to her would be a wondrous, temporary thing? With or without the class difference, he rarely remained devoted to a woman for very long. With the wide social gap that lay between him and Roxy, wouldn't that happen even more quickly than usual?

He supposed there was only one way to find out.

"Then we'll just have to bridge that 'social thing,' as you call it," he told her.

His response seemed to surprise her. She still met his gaze levelly, but she blinked, once, twice, three times, like a wind-up toy.

"What?" she asked.

"I said we'll have to do something to close the cultural gap that's lying between us. If you ask me, it's not nearly as wide as you seem to think, anyway."

"Why do you say that?"

For the first time since they had begun their conversation, Spencer took a few meaningful strides into the living room.

He paused by his desk and lifted up the file folder that housed the facts of his life, then idly thumbed through the documents inside.

"Just that maybe I'm not so far from you as you think."

"Spencer…"

"Roxy, I'm no different from you or anyone else. You're wrong about money making people do funny things." He held up the file in his hand. "If I'd grown up Steve McCormick, I'd still be a lot like I am now. I might dress differently, and speak differently, and have a different job, but I'd still be the same person."

"No, you wouldn't."

"Yes, I would."

"You'll never convince me of that."

"At least give me the opportunity to try."

"Why? Spencer, what's the point?" She stood and paced restlessly to the side of the room farthest from him. "This thing between us, whatever it is, will never work. I'm telling you we're just too different."

"And I'm telling you we're not."

When she said nothing more to contradict him, he took advantage of her silence. "Please, Roxy. Just give it a chance. Give *me* a chance. Let me into your life for a while, and I'll let you into mine. And you'll see that they're not as different as you think."

She eyed him thoughtfully for a moment, seeming to ponder his suggestion. Finally, she began to make her way slowly back toward him, little by little closing the distance she had put between them, both literally and, he hoped, figuratively.

"Okay," she said. "We'll give it a chance. But I'm telling you right now it'll never—"

"Roxy."

"What?"

He closed what little space remained between them and cupped his hands over her shoulders. But he didn't pull her against him, as he wanted to do. He simply gave her shoulders

a brief squeeze, then stroked his palms down her arms and
held her hands loosely in his.

"If you go into it with that attitude," he said softly, "then
you're right. It'll never work."

She uttered an impatient sound. "All right, all right. We'll
give it a chance. Period."

He smiled, squeezed her fingers lightly with his, then reluctantly let go of them. "You won't be sorry."

"That remains to be seen."

Instead of acknowledging her pessimism, Spencer tried
again. "So where do we start?"

She grinned at him, but the expression was in no way jovial. "You can start by taking me home," she told him.

He grinned back. "Great. Where do you live?"

"But this is your office," Spencer said as he and Roxy
pulled his Porsche to a stop in front of the crumbling brick
building where it had all begun.

"Yup. It sure is," she told him, waiting for the outburst
she was certain would follow.

He studied her from the driver's seat, his expression puzzled. "But I asked you for directions to your house. Your
home."

"This is my home."

He narrowed his eyes at her. "You actually *live* in your
office?"

She nodded.

"Why?"

She shrugged and replied honestly, "It's all I can afford
right now."

"But—"

"I own the space, thanks to Bingo. It's the only thing I *do*
own. That and the furnishings inside and the clothes on my
back. All of whose luxury you've witnessed for yourself,"
she added meaningfully.

"But—"

"Come on up. I'll fix us some breakfast."

Before he could object, she opened the passenger side door

and scrambled out of the car. She was halfway up the interior stairs when he caught up with her, and she supposed that was because he had to take a couple of minutes to activate the car's alarm.

Fat lot of good that was going to do, she thought. On this street, his car could be stripped clean before the alarm even sputtered to life, the alarm itself becoming part of the booty. This *was* a professional neighborhood, after all.

"You like waffles?" she asked over her shoulder as she topped the stair that brought them to the third floor.

"Yes."

"Good."

She fished her key out of her shoulder bag and unlocked her office door, then made her way to a small refrigerator in the corner. She plucked out a plastic bag of what should have been frozen waffles, but which were actually half-defrosted waffles, due to the dubious nature of her freezer. She shook a few free of the wrapping, tossed them into a prehistoric-looking toaster oven, then punched the button four times before it stuck enough to get the contraption working.

"Normally, I'd wash up in the bathroom down the hall while those were toasting—it usually takes at least three punches of the toaster button and a good fifteen minutes before those puppies are done—but since you were kind enough to let me use your facilities this morning, that won't be necessary."

Spencer said nothing, just continued to watch her hasty movements around the office in silence. Roxy reached for a plastic basket on top of the fridge, riffled through its contents for a moment, then snagged a couple of small plastic containers of syrup from the assortment of fast-food-issue condiment packets nestled there.

"I always grab more than I need whenever I eat out," she said in reference to the containers she placed on top of the radiator. "Sorry, but these won't get as hot as they should. I usually leave them on the radiator all night if I know I'm going to need them in the morning."

"Roxy—"

"Excuse me while I change my clothes."

Before he could stop her, she strode quickly to a small coat closet opposite the refrigerator and began to sort through the meager collection of garments that was her wardrobe. Since she'd be meeting with a new client today, she opted for a pair of black trousers, a white shirt and a dark blue jacket.

"Be right back," she sang out with false cheeriness as she stepped inside the closet and closed the door behind her.

When she emerged, she found Spencer still standing in the middle of the room staring at her, just as he had been before. Although he had assured her he was taking the day off to experience her life with her, he had dressed as if for work, in yet another dark, sleekly designed, very expensive suit.

But instead of making him look like a tightly bound, conservative businessman, the ensemble seemed to barely contain the wildness she knew was housed within. That spark of fierce savagery of which she now knew him capable seemed to burn brighter than before somehow. His blue eyes seemed darker, more mysterious, more passionate than they had been the first time he had entered her office. He seemed less a man focused on business and more a man focused on the joys of life.

He seemed a little more like Roxy herself.

"I think the waffles are ready," he said blandly when she exited the closet. "If you call charred black and smoking ready."

She noted the acrid smell of burning waffle just as he completed his statement and rushed to the toaster oven, gaping at the ugly mess that greeted her. "What? How'd that happen? It's never done that before." She picked up the appliance and shook it hard. "Damned seventies manufacturing. This thing couldn't be more than twenty-five years old. Where's the pride that used to go into craftsmanship?"

"Why don't we just go out for breakfast?" Spencer suggested.

She shook her head. "No, you wanted to lead *my* life, remember? And *I* never go out for breakfast."

Gingerly, he picked up one of the plastic syrup containers, dangling it between thumb and forefinger. "Oh, no?"

She dipped her head in acknowledgment. "Okay. Occasionally, I eat breakfast out. When I'm on a case, or when I'm running late."

"You're on a case now," he reminded her.

"Yeah, but the money from the guy's retainer has run out."

"So tell him to pay you what he owes you for work completed."

Roxy shrugged. "Okay. Give me a minute to make up his bill."

Hastily, she consulted the notebook where she logged her hours and expenses, did some figuring in her head, scratched some numbers onto a pad, then double-checked them before she handed the scrap of paper to Spencer. He scanned the information for accuracy and, evidently satisfied she wasn't trying to rip him off, removed an eel-skin checkbook from his inside jacket pocket, wrote a check and handed it back. Roxy thanked him, noted the amount to make sure *he* wasn't ripping *her* off, then folded the check neatly in half and deposited it into her shirt pocket.

"Okay, breakfast is on me," she said with a smile. "First stop, the bank. Then Denny's."

Spencer nodded. "Whatever you normally do."

"Well, Denny's is actually living high, but what the hell. I just got paid."

He smiled at her. "Then let's go."

Outside the building, he hesitated by his car, but Roxy continued to walk steadfastly down the street.

"Roxy!" he called after her.

She spun around. "What?"

He seemed mystified by her behavior. "Where are you going?"

"To the bus stop."

"Why?"

She rolled her eyes heavenward as she walked back to where he stood on the sidewalk. "My life, remember?" she asked. "I take the bus. Or the metro when the bus won't go where I need to go."

"But I have my car."

She arched her eyebrows philosophically. "Your car isn't part of my life."

"But—"

"Look, the F bus runs like clockwork. We've got maybe two minutes before it arrives on yon corner." She began to walk backward in the direction she had followed before. "You coming?"

He looked longingly at his car, as if it were the last time he would ever see it in his life. Roxy decided he was probably pretty justified in his feelings. Then, very, very reluctantly, he tucked his keys back into his trouser pocket and, very, very slowly, he followed her.

Ultimately, they had to run to catch the bus, but because Manny the driver knew Roxy so well and, more importantly, liked her, he didn't play bus tag the way he did for most of the people who had to make a run for it. As the bus lurched forward, Roxy and Spencer stumbled to the back and found separate seats.

Roxy's was next to an elegantly attired elderly woman who wore white gloves, smelled faintly of lilacs and had a nice smile. Spencer's was beside a man expounding quite loudly to no one in particular about the hierarchy of angels. When the man came to the Powers in the second circle, he grew quite agitated and began to wave his arms about frantically. He only hit Spencer once, but it was a sound punch to the shoulder. As politely as he could, Spencer rose, moved to the aisle and evidently decided to stand instead beside Roxy.

"Does this happen often?" he asked quietly.

She smiled. "Raymond is harmless. He just gets stuck on the Powers sometimes." She leaned back in her seat and shouted back to the man, "Principalities, Raymond! The Principalities come next! Move on to the third circle already, will ya?" When she looked at Spencer again, her smile softened some. "That ought to do it."

He eyed her cryptically, but she had no idea what he was thinking.

"This is my life, Spencer," she said softly. "Take it or leave it."

She wasn't sure, but she thought he nodded. "Oh, I'll take it. For now. But I'm going to get my chance, too, you know."

She was about to ask him what he meant by that, but Manny slammed on the brakes to avoid hitting a bicycle messenger who came out of nowhere, and Spencer went tumbling forward on his hands and knees.

"I'll get my chance," he repeated as he stood and brushed himself off. "Just you wait, Roxy. Just you wait."

Nine

The end of the day found the two of them sitting in a rented Escort outside a warehouse in Foggy Bottom, the chain of events that had led them there erratic, to say the least. Spencer's head was still spinning at what Roxy has assured him was a typical day.

From Denny's, they'd gone to the National Zoo to meet with a man who suspected his wife was not only cheating on him, but also heading up a sophisticated drug smuggling operation with roots in the Amazon jungles. In spite of the fact that the man was clearly a lunatic, Roxy had taken him very seriously and had studiously written down all the man's suspicions—everything from the phone calls he was certain came from Desi Arnaz, who really *wasn't* dead, but who was seeing his wife, to the trip his wife had taken last summer to visit her mother in Walla Walla, which the man was absolutely certain was actually a smuggling excursion to Brazil to trade American-made space heaters for cocaine because, as everyone knew, American-made space heaters were the currency of choice among the South American drug cartel.

From there, the day had only become more bizarre. Roxy had actually researched the man's suspicions through countless phone calls and consultations with even bigger lunatics, a series of interviews and meetings that had ultimately led them to this deserted warehouse, a dark and dangerous-looking place in a dark and dangerous-looking area.

It was after eleven, and Spencer figured it was about time to be winding up this charade to go home and unwind with a warm snifter of brandy and an even warmer snuggle with Roxy. Roxy, however, evidently had other plans.

"You can't possibly think that man's suspicions are valid, can you?" he asked her for perhaps the tenth time that day.

"Of course not," she answered as she had every time. "But he's paying me to make sure, so the least I can do is give the case my fullest attention."

"You realize, of course, that he's a lunatic."

She seemed unconcerned. "So are most of my clients."

He eyed her dubiously.

"Present company excluded," she clarified with a smile when she turned to meet his gaze.

"Thank you."

"You're welcome."

He ran his hand idly over the car dashboard. "I suppose by now my Porsche has been blowtorched into a million little pieces."

She stifled a yawn. "More than likely."

"I really liked that car."

"You'll get another one."

"It won't be the same."

"Maybe you'll like the new one better."

"Maybe…"

"There's more coffee," she told him as she reached for a thermos under the seat.

He held up a hand definitively. "No, thank you. I've had more than enough. I think I can actually feel my skin breathing."

She chuckled, but said nothing.

"Roxy?"

"Hmmm?"

"Are you carrying a gun?"

She turned completely in her seat to look at him, obviously surprised by the change of subject. "No. Why do you ask?"

He shrugged. "This doesn't seem like the safest of places. I thought private investigators always carried weapons."

"Actually, a lot of them don't. That's more a TV thing."

"Really?"

She nodded. "Besides, I don't like guns. Never have. Bingo always had a lot of them stashed in various places. Not because he was a P.I., but because he just liked guns. They always gave me the creeps, though. Statistically speaking, I'm safer without one than I am with one, anyway."

He studied her for a long time, until she seemed to grow uncomfortable with his scrutiny.

"What?" she finally asked. "Why do you keep looking at me like that?"

He shook his head. "You're just such an enigma."

Her eyebrows shot up in surprise. "I'm a what?"

"You're a small woman who talks like a big man. You're in a tough-guy occupation, but you're not a tough guy at all."

"Hey, I'm as tough as they come," she countered indignantly.

He smiled. "No, you're not. You're a softie."

"I am *not* a softie," she assured him. Her voice reeked with contempt, as if in accusing her of being gentle he'd just insulted her in the foulest way possible. After a moment, she added, "I bet I could beat you at arm wrestling."

He laughed out loud. "No, you couldn't."

"Twenty bucks says I can."

"You're on."

Without encouragement, she shoved up the sleeve of her jacket and shirt and propped her elbow soundly on the armrest between the two bucket seats. Spencer knew he was way too wired if he had just agreed to arm wrestle a woman who probably weighed half as much as he did. Nevertheless, the glitter of combat in her eyes taunted him, so he pushed up his own sleeve and settled his elbow beside hers, gripping her hand firmly in his own.

"Ready?" he asked her.

"I was born ready."

"On the count of three..."

They made the count together, and within five seconds of completing it, Spencer had not only pinned Roxy's arm to his seat, but had punctuated his victory by reaching over and hauling her across the armrest to land in his lap.

"You owe me twenty bucks," he told her.

"I'll deduct it from my expenses."

"You do that."

In the darkness, he could barely make out her features, but her eyes reflected the scant light from the moon, and he could hear her breath moving rapidly in and out of her lungs. A single dark strand of hair had fallen across her forehead, and without even thinking about what he was doing, he lifted a hand to thumb it back into place. Then he dropped his fingertips to her mouth and traced her lips with a feather-light touch, wanting badly to kiss her, but happy, too, just to be this close.

Roxy didn't move, but simply gazed up at him in the darkness. Her skin was warm where he touched her, supple, yielding. Her show of toughness in daring him to arm wrestle her had ultimately had the opposite effect. Instead of displaying her rough-and-readiness, it had simply reinforced her softness, her sensuality. Instead of insisting that Spencer back off, which he suspected she had intended to do, her challenge had invited him to delve further. And he wasn't such an idiot that he'd decline an invitation like that.

As he bent his head to hers, he tightened his hold on her back, cupped his hand at the base of her scalp and lifted her up to meet his kiss. As their lips touched, Roxy buried her fingers in his hair, holding his head in place, silently urging him closer. At first he only rubbed her lips gently with his, pulling back before lowering his head again. This time, when he covered her mouth with his, it was with a bit more pressure. He traced the delicate contours of her lips with his tongue, nipped at the lower one with his teeth, then covered her mouth completely with his.

What ensued was a battle. Roxy vied with him over who could most effectively plunder whom. The kiss was more a war for complete possession than it was a gesture of subtle exploration. It was almost as if they were trying to prove who was more desperate, more deserving, more alone. In the long run, Spencer decided it must be a draw.

He pulled her closer to him still, their chests pressed together, their hearts beating rapid-fire against each other. The hand cupped at her nape tangled in her hair, and he looped his other arm around her waist as if he never intended to let her go. He felt one warm hand on his jaw, another squeezing his upper arm. Their breathing began to come in quick, erratic gasps, the sounds oddly rhythmic in spite of their irregularity.

He dropped a hand to her waist and tugged her shirt free of her trousers, then began to unfasten the buttons one by one. He had just freed the one at her neck when a loud, dull thumping on the roof of the car forced them to spring apart.

The windows, he noted much to his dismay, were fogged up enough that he couldn't quite make out the shady figure standing outside the driver's side window. Nor could he tell, thanks to the bright ring of light offered from the figure's flashlight, if the figure was alone or part of a gang.

That was only one realization that didn't set well with him. Another was that he and Roxy were still quite alone in a place that was anything but safe. But most of all, Spencer realized that when he got right down to it, he didn't care about any of those things. Didn't care about his own personal safety or Roxy's. All he wanted was for whomever had rapped on the car to go away and let them indulge in what they were doing before being so rudely interrupted, safe surroundings or no safe surroundings.

"Let me handle this," Roxy said as she hastily began to refasten the buttons on her shirt.

"But—"

"Let me handle it," she repeated, her tone of voice indicating she would gladly throttle him if he didn't follow her lead.

The rap on the roof of the car sounded again, shaking the little vehicle as if it were a small insect. Roxy smoothed her hands through her hair and turned to roll down the window.

"Do you think that's wise…?" Spencer began to ask, but cut off the question when he saw the expression she threw back at him. All right, all right, he replied mentally. He'd behave himself. For now.

Roxy finished rolling down the window and, despite the darkness surrounding the figure on the other side and the bright light shining in her face, made out a gray rent-a-cop shirt on the other side. Its dull fabric strained at the tarnished silver buttons over a larger-than-could-ever-hope-to-be-a-real-policeman belly, and a chubby hand was settled resolutely on the butt of the pistol still snapped into its holster. She marveled that the guy had lasted more than five minutes on the job, doing things like going up to a suspicious vehicle in an area like this and pounding on the roof without even unfastening his holster, let alone calling for backup.

Idly, Roxy further noted the presence of a wedding band on the fourth finger of his left hand and wondered if his wife would mind so much being a widow, as the poor woman likely would be in the very near future.

"Is there a problem, Officer?" she rattled off in her best gosh-I'm-just-a-dumb-female voice. Before he had a chance to answer, she quickly continued, "This isn't a no-parking zone, is it? I hate it when I do that. I did that once, and my car got towed. It was so embarrassing. I looked for signs—I always do that now—but I didn't see any. I'm not in any kind of trouble, am I? My husband will get really steamed at me if I do something like that again. It cost eighty dollars to get the car out of…what do you call it? Impounding, that's it. Can you imagine? Eighty dollars!"

The security guard lowered his flashlight some, then bent to place one hand on his knee and stare in through the open window. He couldn't have been more than twenty-one years old, Roxy thought. He was probably a newlywed, and had taken this job to moonlight in an effort to help make ends meet. Maybe he and his wife were saving up for a house, or to have a baby.

And why she cared enough to be spinning fanciful tales about some guy who was going to cause her trouble, Roxy thought even further, she couldn't begin to imagine.

"Ma'am," the young man began, "what're you doin' here?"

She feigned confusion. "I'm sitting in my car with, um…" She let her voice trail off for a telling moment, then continued, "With…my, uh, my…I mean…that is…my friend. Yeah, that's it. My friend." More forcefully, she repeated, "I'm sitting in my car with my friend. Is that a crime, Officer?"

For the first time, the guard looked farther into the car, shining his light right in Spencer's face. To his credit, Spencer said nothing, just squinted at the man, inclined his head forward silently, then leaned back in his seat, into the shadows. The guard turned the light outward again and focused his attention back on Roxy.

"Your friend?" he repeated. "Isn't something like *that* gonna cause you more trouble with your husband than a parking violation?"

She smiled at him. "You've obviously never met my husband."

"No, ma'am," the young man answered. "Obviously I haven't."

"Well, then, if that's all…?" She began to roll her window up again.

"No, ma'am, that's not all."

She rolled her window back down and gazed at him expectantly.

The security guard sighed, clearly exasperated and wishing he were somewhere else. "This is private property, ma'am. No one's supposed to be here this time of night except me. How did you get through the security gate?"

She shot her eyebrows up in confusion. "What security

gate? I don't recall seeing a security gate." She turned to Spencer. "Bob? Did you see a security gate?"

He shook his head, but said nothing, and she sensed that was because he was getting really, really mad.

She turned back to the night watchman. "Bob didn't see a security gate, either. Are you sure you have one?"

The man sighed again. "Do you have any ID?" he asked instead of responding to her question.

Roxy went through the motions as she pretended to search first her purse, then her pockets, then the glove compartment for her driver's license, all the while complaining about Americans no longer being free, thanks to the current administration's policy of turning this country into a police state and how dare he question her integrity and what was wrong with getting away from it all once in a while with a friend and blah blah blah blah blah.

When she finally handed over her driver's license to the night watchman, he flashed his light on it, then gripped it between his thumb and forefinger. "Ms. McCormick—"

"*Mrs.* McCormick," she corrected him, feeling Spencer stiffen beside her when he realized she had just identified herself with the name of his missing twin sister.

"Mrs. McCormick," the guard began again, "if you'll just wait right here, I have to go make a phone call."

"Of course I'll wait right here," she assured him. "Where else would I go? Bob and I were just discussing this new foreign policy the president has introduced. What's *your* opinion on that? I think it's outrageous that—"

"Excuse me, ma'am."

He shook his head and palmed her ID, then turned his back to the car. The moment he was out of sight, Roxy ground the vehicle to life and sped off in a cloud of exhaust and hastily spewed gravel. At the security gate, she slid her aluminum-foil-covered Visa card through the sensor, and the chain-link fence slowly slid open for them.

"Honestly," she muttered as she drove through, "how anyone can be surprised at how rampant industrial espionage has become is beyond me. Especially when everyone seems to be buying their security equipment from Mattel these days.''

Spencer didn't say a word until they were well away from Foggy Bottom and entering Dupont Circle. And when he did speak again, she realized he had been saving quite a lot up to tell her.

"Just what the hell was all that about?" he asked the moment the red neon lights for the Brickskellar came into view. "Do you realize how many laws we just broke back there? Do you realize how easy it's going to be to find us, thanks to this bumper car you rented? Do you realize what this is going to do to my position in the community? Do you realize we could both wind up in jail? Do you realize that man is going to swear out a warrant for the arrest of my sister?"

"Do you realize how hysterical you sound?" she retorted as she jerked the little car to a halt and backed into a space by the curb that anyone less adventurous would have passed right by.

He snapped his mouth shut and glared at her.

She threw the gearshift into park and turned in her seat to face him. "*You* were the one who wanted to tag along with me in my life, remember? Now will you just relax and let me do my job?"

"Relax? With you?" he exclaimed. "How can anyone be relaxed around you? I never know what you're going to do next."

"Impetuous is my middle name, okay? Get used to it."

"Roxy—"

"Spencer, nothing is going to happen to us. For one thing, that guy was either too new at the job or too indifferent to it to even care whether or not we ever get caught. As far as he's concerned, I'm some bored, lonely housewife from Silver Spring who's getting even with her husband for something by seeing some sleazy guy in some lurid, degrading setting."

He began to object at the role into which she had cast him, but she continued on quickly before he had the chance. "He'll probably throw the driver's license away. Even if he does make out a report of the incident—which I'm telling you is *highly* unlikely—Charlotte McCormick doesn't exist. She's someone else now. No one is going to arrest your sister."

"But—"

"And he never even bothered to get the license plate number from the car, so you and I are safe, too. Not that I used my real name to rent this sucker, anyway. What kind of novice do you take me for?"

"But what if, when you go to turn the car in, the cops are waiting for us?"

She shook her head at him hopelessly. "Who says I'm turning this car in?"

"Roxy!"

"Oh, chill out. They'll find it. Eventually."

"Sure, stripped to the framework."

She glanced out the window. "No way. We're on Embassy Row. This place is more heavily guarded and watched than the White House. It'll be fine."

He studied her doubtfully.

"Will you please just trust me?"

He neither agreed nor disagreed with her request. He only continued to stare at her as if he had no idea how to proceed.

So Roxy took the initiative. "C'mon, let's go have a beer."

Without awaiting his reply, she tucked the key under the floor mat and exited the car, slamming the door shut behind her and making sure it was locked. After a moment, Spencer opened the door on the passenger side and climbed out, stretching his large frame from shoulder to calf once he was on the sidewalk. Roxy watched his motions with fascination. Jeez, even in a business suit, the guy was gorgeous. Not soft and cheesy looking, the way most businessmen looked, to her way of thinking, but hard and sturdy and sexy as hell.

And why did she continue to think about him that way, she demanded of herself *again*, when any future the two of them had was nonexistent?

The Brickskellar was one of the few places in D.C. that catered to an upscale clientele where Roxy actually felt comfortable. Its dark interior and bare brick walls made her feel at home for some reason. And the beer selection was extraordinary. Even an upright guy like Spencer should be able to find *something* to suit his taste here.

"May I see a wine list?" he asked the waiter once they were seated.

Both Roxy and the waiter looked at him, horrified.

"What?" he asked in response to their expressions. "What's wrong?"

"This place has a hundred and fifty brands of beer to choose from," Roxy told him. "It's kind of the reason people come here. To drink beer."

"I don't drink beer," he replied in a matter-of-fact tone of voice.

"My life, Spencer," she reminded him.

He growled his accession. "All right. What do you recommend?"

She smiled at him. "Shall I order for us both?" she asked prettily. At least, she hoped it was prettily. She'd never much striven for pretty at anything before.

"Please do," he told her through gritted teeth.

The waiter turned to Roxy, who ordered her usual Anchor Steam for herself, and a nice imported French number for Spencer. "It has a lovely bouquet," she told him when their server departed. "Flirtatious without being bold, subtle, but still playful. A nice, yeasty flavor that rolls right off the tongue. *Beer Observer* magazine rated it a 91."

"Very funny," Spencer muttered.

"What's the matter?" she asked him. "Beginning to feel uncomfortable with the way I live?"

He shook his head. "No. But you seem to be going to an awful lot of trouble to try and make me feel uncomfortable."

His assertion was ridiculous, of course, but Roxy said nothing in response.

"So what are you going to tell your client?" he asked when the silence began to become uneasy.

She shrugged. "The truth. That the warehouse he was certain housed a huge cache of cocaine actually contains school supplies, that in spite of an exhaustive search, I found no evidence to indicate that his wife is having an affair with Desi Arnaz or anyone else, and that her trip home to Walla Walla was just that. A trip home.''

"And do you think that will be enough for him?''

She shook her head. "No. I think as soon as he gets off the phone with me, he'll be on the phone with another private investigator, hiring him or her to look into the matter. People like that are never satisfied until they have their worst suspicions confirmed.''

"Sounds a lot like someone else I know.''

Her gaze flew up to lock with his, and she narrowed her eyes suspiciously. "What's that supposed to mean?''

Before he could answer, the waiter returned with their beers, and Roxy decided it might be better to just let the question go unanswered. Instead, she turned the topic back to Spencer's case.

"Look, speaking of cases, I need to know how you want me to proceed with yours.''

He swallowed a mouthful of beer, made a surprised, agreeable face and looked at the label. "I want you to find my sister. I thought you knew that.''

"I do. But have you really considered everything that's going to involve?''

He levered his gaze to meet hers. "It means I'll find my sister. I'll have my family back together.''

"But what if your sister doesn't want to be found?''

His expression was completely dumbfounded. "Of course she wants to be found. Why wouldn't she?''

Roxy sighed. She wasn't particularly familiar with morality, having never given the subject much thought, but she knew there were moral implications to what Spencer wanted her to do, and she doubted he'd considered them any more than she normally did. In spite of that, she thought it was important for him to realize just exactly what he might be putting in motion here, and to be prepared for what might happen as a result.

"What if she doesn't even know she was adopted?'' Roxy asked him. "What if her parents never told her?''

"Don't you think that's unlikely? Most adoptive parents explain adoption to their children as soon as those children are old enough to understand. It's just the right thing to do."

"But what if her parents never did? What if she's used to being part of a family that's the only family she's ever known or ever cared to know? What's going to happen when she finds out about her past life, however brief it was?"

Spencer just looked at her, and didn't respond.

"I mean, look how deeply this whole thing has affected you, and you *wanted* to uncover this information. You *wanted* to find out the truth. How would you feel if this was something you discovered by accident, because some total stranger came to your door one day and said, 'Hey, guess what? You're not who you think you are.'"

Still, Spencer said nothing in response.

"And even if she does know she's adopted, there's still a very real possibility that she has no desire whatever to delve into a past she doesn't even remember. Something like this can really mess with a person's head, Spencer. At best, she's going to be shaken up. At worst, she might be driven to seek counseling. And in either case, she may very well want nothing to do with you. Are you sure you want to do that to your sister? To yourself?"

He took another swallow of beer and let his gaze settle on something over Roxy's right shoulder. She was certain that no matter what he was looking at, he was seeing something else entirely. She remained silent and let him think, sipping her beer as she watched the gears turn.

Finally, he focused on her face again, his expression heavy and not a little grim. "Call me a selfish bastard," he said, "but I still want you to find her. Then, if she wants to rebuke me, she can. I just want her to know I'm here for her. And I want to meet her. At least once."

Roxy sighed, not certain the decision he'd made was a good one, but professionally obligated to see this thing through to its conclusion.

"She's my sister, Roxy," he stated unnecessarily. "My *twin* sister. We shared a womb. We received nourishment together. We experienced birth together. The same spark that gave me life gave it to her. And something tells me that if I've been so certain of her existence all my life, she's been equally certain of mine. I want you to find her. Please.''

Roxy sighed, but nodded. ''Okay, Spencer. I'll find her for you. Whatever happens after that is up to you.''

He smiled, but she wasn't sure whether he was happy about her assurance that she would find his sister, or about something else entirely. Somehow, she got the feeling his satisfaction came on a couple of levels.

''Great,'' he finally said. ''Because I have big plans, Roxy. Very big plans.''

Ten

Spencer's foray into Roxy's daily life ended in much the same way as it had begun. When they finally returned to her office sometime after 3:00 a.m., they discovered that instead of being stripped, his car had been stolen completely. Two hookers had affixed their platform shoes to the stairs that led to her building, then sneered at Roxy for invading their turf before assuring Spencer *they* could do whatever *she* could do, only better and for a much more reasonable price. The junkie who had collapsed in the doorway posed yet another obstacle, so Roxy suggested maybe she and Spencer would be better off doing what she normally did on those very few occasions when she was forced to return home so late—go up the fire escape and slip through the window instead.

After she jimmied the window and climbed through, she turned to thank him for seeing her home safely and send him on his way, only to discover that he had crawled through the opening behind her.

"Aren't you going home?" she asked him.

He gaped at her as he brushed himself off. "What, and leave you here by yourself? Are you crazy?"

"I'm here by myself every night, Spencer."

"Not tonight, you aren't."

She opened her mouth to object, to tell him that his day in her life was over now, but the look in his eye stopped her. No matter what she said, she knew he wasn't going anywhere. In spite of that, she offered halfheartedly, "There's nowhere for you to sleep. I crash on the couch in the outer office. There's barely room for me there. No way will we both fit."

"I'll sleep on the floor."

"But—"

He pulled the window closed and latched it tight, double-checking the lock before turning back to face her. When he did, his expression was no more agreeable than his tone of voice. "Believe it or not, Roxy, it won't be the first time in my life I've slept on the floor."

She couldn't help baiting him. "Oh, sure, not if you want to count camping out in your bedroom when you were a kid, with your Patagonia sleeping bag and Biff and Margo from the next mansion over."

He frowned at her. "How about sleeping on the floor of a holding cell in a federal facility? Does that count?"

Her eyebrows shot up at that. "A holding cell? By the feds?"

He made a sour face as he recalled the memory of many years ago. "I would have taken the cot," he added, "but it was already occupied by a cross-dresser with pierced nipples who was wanted on some kind of federal pornography charge. Call me overly cautious, but I thought it best to keep my distance."

Roxy continued to stare at him for a moment, then finally snapped herself out of her stupor. "You did time in a federal facility? For what?"

He rubbed the bridge of his nose and squeezed his eyes shut. "I didn't actually do time. Just one night. It was really all a mistake. I fit the description of a man they wanted for murder. Once they checked out my alibi and realized who I was, they released me.''

Roxy could only stare at him. ''You were mistaken for a murderer? You actually did time in jail because the feds thought you iced somebody?''

''I told you I didn't actually *do time*, as you so Chandler-esquely put it,'' he insisted. ''But it just goes to prove what I've been telling you all along.''

''What's that?''

''That you and I have more in common than you think.''

She expelled an indignant breath of air. ''Like hell we do. *I've* never spent the night in the can. Wow. You just never know about some people, do you?''

He dropped his fists to his hips and glared at her. ''The only reason *you've* never been incarcerated is because you've never been caught. I, on the other hand, never broke the law—until I met you, of course—but still wound up in jail. Don't you think there's some kind of bizarre relationship there?''

''Okay, okay,'' she relented. ''Maybe. I'm sorry. It's just that I'm having all kinds of trouble visualizing you sleeping on the concrete floor of a human cage, that's all.''

''It was very unpleasant.''

She smiled. ''I'll bet.''

He gazed down at her floor. ''Much like this will be, I'm sure.''

''You could always go home.''

He shook his head and met her gaze levelly. ''Not without you, I can't.''

She said nothing in response. Instead, she spent an extraordinary amount of energy trying to convince herself that she hadn't heard what, for a moment, had sounded like an implied meaning behind his words. There was no way he could have been trying to tell her what she could almost let herself believe he had been trying to tell her. All he had said was that he wasn't returning to his house tonight unless she was going with him.

He hadn't said a word about his home not being a home unless she was there with him. Had he?

You are being such *a jerk,* she told herself. *Stop it right now, before you do something* really *stupid.*

"You can have the blanket and pillow, at least," she told him quietly. "I won't need them. It's a warm night, anyway. That ought to help some."

"What would help is you coming home with me. Now."

He shrugged out of his jacket and loosened his necktie, then yanked his shirttail free of his trousers and unfastened the buttons on the cuffs and halfway down the front. He rolled up his sleeves, toed off his Gucci loafers and raked his hands through his hair in exhaustion. And all Roxy could think was that he was beginning to look less and less like a rich, workaholic businessman, and more like a rampantly sexy guy she would love to get to know better.

Of course, she already knew him better, she reminded herself. Thanks to that little cha-cha lesson at his house the night before. Briefly, she considered seducing him her way now that he was here on her turf, but quickly dismissed the idea. Why make things worse than they already were?

She strode to the closet that doubled as her dressing room and tugged a blanket and pillow down from the top shelf. Wordlessly, she spun around and tossed them to Spencer, who caught them quite capably and just as silently. He eyed her expectantly, and she remembered that she hadn't yet responded to his last remark. Fine, she thought to herself. Let him lose sleep over her answer. God knew she probably would.

"Sweet dreams," she said instead as she grabbed her toothbrush and nightclothes from the closet. Without further comment, she pushed past him and through the door that led to the outer office.

Only when she closed the door behind herself did she realize she had been holding her breath, and she took some comfort in the soft *click* of the latch as it caught. She heard a few quiet rustles from the other side as Spencer made up his bed, then she went down the hall to the women's room to brush her teeth.

When she returned, she took off her own jacket and shoes and unbuttoned her own shirt in exactly the same way Spencer had only moments ago. Then she forsook her nightwear and stretched out on the sofa still dressed, with one forearm resting on her forehead in exactly the same way she had seen him sleeping the night before. And she wondered how on earth he could think the two of them had anything in common at all.

Spencer leaned lazily in the doorway that linked inner office to outer office and watched Roxy for a long time before waking her. The scant rays of early-morning sunlight barely reached the outer office from the dirty windows in the other room, but even in the hazy grayness, he could tell she still slept deeply. She lay on her back, her head turned slightly to the side toward him, with one hand dangling over the side of the couch, fingers skimming the floor. The other hand rested half-curled over her belly, and he realized that this was the first time he'd ever seen her completely relaxed.

Even when she'd slept with him at his house, she hadn't slept this deeply. He'd felt her moving around most of the night, and she'd uttered soft sounds in her sleep that were anything but easy and untroubled. Only here in her office—her home—was Roxy comfortable enough to surrender completely to slumber. And when she was like this, something about her changed.

Gone was the phony edge she adopted to keep people at a distance. Gone were the sharp retorts she used to deflect any kind of dialogue that might become too uncomfortably intimate. Gone was the wall she had erected shortly after he'd met her that had prevented him from seeing too deeply inside her soul.

Instead, she lay open and uninhibited, relaxed and easy. Her shirt buttons were undone far enough down that he could see the champagne lace of her brassiere peeking out from beneath the fabric. Her cheeks were stained pink, her lashes thick and sooty against them, her lips slightly parted as if she'd needed extra oxygen at some point during the night.

Spencer hoped that was because she'd been having the same kind of dreams that had taunted him all night, the kind that made him gasp for air and wake up all sweaty and full of wanting. The kind that overshadowed everything that had come before, and anything the future might hold. The kind that made him want to forget about all but the immediate moment. Forget about all but Roxy.

But he had plans for the day. He had plans for her. With a few silent strides, he approached the couch and extended his hand toward her face, to brush the backs of his fingers softly across her cheek.

Still sleeping, she turned her head toward his hand and uttered a quiet sigh. Then she parted her lips more and whispered, "Spencer."

The way she said his name made his flesh grow warm and his belly catch fire. He curled his fingers tightly into his palm, then flexed them forcefully again. With the tip of his fingers, he gently rubbed her lower lip and said softly, "Roxy."

She turned her head again, this time shifting her body in the process, and a length of dark hair fell across her cheek. Spencer brushed it back in place, threading his fingers through her hair, marveling at how it, too, seemed to be warm and alive. He curled one strand around his index finger, then knelt beside the couch. Still clutching the dark tress, he opened his hand over her jaw and touched his lips to hers.

Roxy melted into him. There was no other way to describe the gesture. One moment their mouths were apart, and the next they were one. Spencer could no more tell where his lips separated from hers than he could predict the future. He only knew that something in Roxy spoke to something inside him, and he was helpless not to answer her when she called out to him the way she was now, the way she had been doing nearly since the moment they'd met. He felt a sharp need for her, and knew somehow that she needed him, too. He only wished he knew what to do, what to say, to make her understand that neither of them had to be alone anymore.

Still not certain how to go about that, he simply took her lips more fully with his, tracing them with the tip of his tongue before delving more deeply inside her. Her warmth enveloped him, her sweetness delighted him. Tasting Roxy was like enjoying a long summer day. The kiss made him feel languid and easy and in no hurry to see it end. So he took it even further, cupping her jaw with both hands, losing his fingers in the softness of the hair at her temples, teasing her lips with his tongue.

And Roxy only turned more toward him, covered his hands with hers, tangled her tongue with his and kissed him harder. Deeper. Faster.

Until she awoke. For one wild moment, even fully awake, she continued to kiss him with fierce, unrestrained audacity. Then, when she realized what she was doing, she quickly jerked her face away from his. For a long time, she only gazed at him with bewildered, still-sleepy eyes. Then she inhaled a ragged breath, swept a shaky hand through her hair and exhaled in fits and starts.

"Wh-what are you doing?" she finally said, her voice scarcely a whisper.

"Trying to wake you up," he told her honestly.

She struggled to a sitting position and pushed her other hand through her hair beside the first one. "You picked a hell of a way to do it."

He shrugged, but made no move to stand. Instead, he looped an arm across her legs and tucked his hand beneath her thigh, curling his fingers possessively into the soft flesh beneath her trousers. "Felt right at the time."

When her gaze met his, her eyes were round and dark. In the dim light, he couldn't quite make out her expression, but the raggedness of her breathing pretty much told him what he needed to know. That she was feeling the same way he was at the moment. Confused. Agitated. Restive.

Aroused.

"*You* feel right, Roxy," he told her further. "All the time."

She shook her head. "You're nuts."

He laughed low but felt in no way funny. "Maybe I am. But then, you only do business with lunatics, right?"

She said nothing in response.

He dropped his voice a notch lower. "Therefore I must fit perfectly into your life."

"Spencer…"

"Now we'll just have to see how well you fit into mine."

That seemed to stump her, because she never finished whatever it was she had wanted to say. He smiled and pushed himself slowly to standing, then gazed down at her for a moment without speaking. She still looked rumpled and tumbled and sexy as hell. And he still wanted her. Badly. But there was something they needed to clear up before they could carry on the way he intended for them to carry on.

"Get dressed," he instructed her as he turned to collect his things from the other room. "We're going to breakfast. But today, we're doing things my way."

Spencer felt a lot better an hour later, standing in front of his stove as he folded one half of a Spanish omelet over the other before expertly transferring it to a plate. Roxy sat at the kitchen table behind him, no more talkative now than she had been since their odd verbal exchange earlier that morning.

They had taken a taxi back to his place and were currently awaiting the arrival of the rental car his insurance carrier would be providing while they looked into the matter of his stolen Porsche. He was showered and shaved and dressed for work, and looking forward to the day with an anticipation he hadn't experienced for a very long time. Because today he'd be doing something different, something he'd never done before. Today, he'd be sharing his day—his life—with Roxy Matheny.

"So…you have breakfast like this every morning?" she asked when he slid the plate to the table beside the thermal coffee carafe.

He had set the table with the dishes that had been in the house since his mother had furnished it for his father decades ago—plain white china and plain clear juice glasses on plain blue place mats, with plain stainless-steel flatware on plain blue napkins. In the center of the table were plain clear salt and pepper shakers and a plain white sugar bowl and cream pitcher. Spencer, however, had added one small, not-so-plain embellishment to the assortment—a slender, sterling-silver vase with a single yellow rose, its petals kissed with pink and just beginning to open to the sun.

"Not really," he confessed. "This is, as you called Denny's yesterday, 'living high.' Usually, I just have a couple of cups of coffee and grab a bagel or something to eat on the way to work. Usually, I'm in a hurry."

She hesitated a moment before asking, "But today you're not?"

He took his seat opposite her. "Today I'm not."

She fingered the rose delicately. "Why the rose?"

He noted her action and smiled. "The rose I added because I thought this was a special occasion."

Her gaze skittered about the room, landing on everything except Spencer. "What kind of special occasion?"

He smiled as he took his seat beside her. "Today is my birthday."

At his announcement, she did meet his gaze again, and he could tell she was making some quick calculations. "That's right…it is your birthday. All this time I've been doing research under your birth date, and it never really occurred to me just how close it was."

He nodded. "It's Charlotte's birthday, too. In years past, I've always wondered what my twin brother was doing on this day. Today, for the first time, I'm wondering about my sister. I'm wondering what she's doing to celebrate. Is her family throwing her a party? Does she have a hot date? Or is she all alone?"

Roxy eyed him thoughtfully. "I doubt very seriously that she's alone on her birthday."

Spencer lifted his coffee to his lips and met her gaze levelly over the rim of his cup. "Don't be so sure."

"Oh, come on. Who spends their birthday alone?"

He sipped his coffee, took his time in swallowing, then answered, "I do."

"You do?"

"Usually. Not today, obviously."

Her expression remained passive, but a flicker of something in her eye told him she wasn't feeling particularly indifferent at the moment. "You mean since your parents died, right?"

He shook his head. "No. Even before their deaths, I generally avoided seeing them on my birthday. I avoided seeing anyone."

"Why?"

He shrugged, as if the answer should be obvious to her. "I wanted to be alone."

She set her own coffee cup down and stared at him. "But why? Why would you want to be alone on your birthday? Even *I* don't spend my birthday alone."

He chose for the moment not to think about what her last statement meant, wonder why she would qualify herself in such a way. Instead, he told her, "Maybe I should clarify that."

"Maybe you should."

"It's not that I *wanted* to be alone on my birthday." He hesitated for a moment, wondering what would be the best way to say what he needed to say. "It was that I wanted to share it with my twin. In some strange way, being alone on my birthday made me feel closer to him. Or, rather, her, as I now know the case to be."

"That psychic connection?" she asked. But this time there was no accusation, no doubt in her voice.

He nodded. "Yes. That psychic connection. I always felt...*close* is the only word I can think of...to my twin on my birthday. That's why I think she must know about me. In some way, whether she's been told the specifics or not, I feel like Charlotte must be as certain that she has a twin as I've always been. And I think she must wonder on her birthday what I'm doing, just as I've always wondered what she's doing."

Roxy nodded in understanding, though Spencer was in no

way certain whether he was making any sense that she could comprehend at all. He had an annual ritual, one that consumed a half hour during the afternoon of every one of his birthdays that he could remember, a brief period of time when he would block himself off completely from the outside world. He'd turn off the phone, darken the room, sit with his eyes closed and concentrate on the twin whose face he couldn't recall. For thirty minutes, he would give his twin his undivided attention, would focus every thought and feeling and desire on that other individual with whom he'd shared the birth of life.

He had no idea if Charlotte had ever felt connected to him in the way he'd always felt connected to her. But part of him knew—part of him was absolutely certain—that she felt his presence in the world somehow. And somehow, some way, he was going to find his way back to her.

"Well...happy birthday," Roxy said, bringing him out of his reverie.

When he looked at her, she had an odd expression on her face. He wasn't quite sure what to make of it. But he told her, "Thank you."

"And thanks for including me in it," she added.

"No thanks necessary."

It would be pointless to tell her that he hadn't given a second thought to spending his birthday with Roxy. For the first time since he was a teenager, he wouldn't be alone on this day, but instead of discomfiting him, the decision seemed to make perfect sense. Including Roxy in his birthday felt as natural as including his twin sister would be. Once he located her.

"We'll find her, Spencer," Roxy told him, seeming to read his mind. "Don't worry about that. It's just a matter of time."

He gazed down into his coffee and saw a distorted image of himself staring back. Himself, only different. A vague, indistinct portrait that looked like him, but wasn't him.

"Thanks, Roxy," he said quietly.

His hand trembled a bit when he spoke, making his reflection in the dark liquid shudder and become nothing but an undulating circle of light. Much like his dream had always been.

They ate breakfast in silence, each seeming to be otherwise occupied with thoughts of something else. And when they were done, Spencer carried their dishes to the dishwasher, loaded it without comment, then turned back to Roxy.

"So..." he asked slowly, both reluctant and anxious to change the subject from his sister's whereabouts to the day ahead. "You ready to be part of a day in *my* life?"

She lifted her coffee cup to her lips and drained its contents. "Do I have a choice?" she asked after she swallowed.

He shook his head. "No."

"Then I guess we may as well get it over with."

"Good. Because I have a point to make, and I'm eager to make it."

Roxy rose, too, her oversize brown mohair sweater falling to her knees over gently faded blue jeans and her ubiquitous hiking boots. "That point being?"

Spencer grinned. "Oh, you're a big girl, Roxy. See if you can figure it out by yourself. You'll have all day, after all."

He strode leisurely back to stand before her and lifted a hand to cup her jaw. Before she could comment on his remark, he bent and pressed his lips to hers, a brief, gentle caress of his mouth over hers that he wanted to take further, but didn't dare.

"And all night, too," he added as he pulled away.

"But—"

"Twenty-four hours," he told her. "That's what I gave to you. That's what you'll give to me."

"But—"

Outside, the honk of a car horn interrupted whatever objection she had been about to utter.

Spencer glanced at his watch. "That will be the car from the insurance company. It's late," he added, eyeing her meaningfully. "Looks like we're going to have to run."

"That guy's a total nut case, you realize that, don't you?" Roxy gazed at Spencer mildly, wondering why on earth he'd even listened to his last appointment for as long as he had. "I mean," she continued, "what he's calling a state-of-the-art trans-Atlantic communications system sounds like it would be about as effective as tying two tomato cans together with the string running under the ocean."

Spencer smiled at her. "You picked up on that, too, did you?"

"Yeah, and I don't know jack about any of this communications technology stuff. Why did you let him go on as long as you did?"

He shrugged. "It's my job. It would have been rude to cut him off in the middle of his presentation. Plus, you never know if there might be some shred of information worth salvaging."

"Why don't you hire someone else to listen to the pitches first? Someone who could at least weed out the psychos?"

He stood and made his way across the sleekly appointed office to the wet bar on the other side of the room. Although much too modern for Roxy's taste, it was impressive. The white walls, minimalist ebony furnishings and stark, bright track lighting were warmed with splashes of red in the geometrically designed area rugs and artwork. The room stated in no uncertain terms how massively high-tech and phenomenally successful this business was, and how forcefully in charge was the man who headed it up.

"Because I'm in charge of research and development," he replied to her question. He lifted a bottle of mineral water in silent query and, when she shook her head no, uncapped it and poured the contents into a slender glass for himself. "Part of what I do is listen to proposals for new technology," he continued. He crossed the room to the black leather sofa whose far right corner she occupied and took a seat beside her.

Roxy arched her brows skeptically. "That was *not* technology," she said, pointing toward the door the man had exited. "That was just silly."

He chuckled. "It happens more often than you might expect. People think they have an idea that's going to revolutionize communications as we know it, only to discover it's been a reality for years now, or would be completely impossible to orchestrate, or else..." His voice trailed off, as if he didn't need to finish his statement.

"Or else what?" she prodded.

He sipped his water. "Or else just plain crazy."

"That's what it was all right."

"Much like some of your clients," he added, gazing over the rim of the glass before taking another not-so-idle sip.

Roxy gazed back. "Meaning what?" Although why she bothered to ask, she had no idea. She pretty much already knew what he was trying to say.

He set his glass down on the surrealistic-looking side table beside the sofa and edged closer to her. "Just that, like you, I deal with a lot of lunatics in my line of work."

She sighed. "So we're back to that, then."

He dropped his hand to her shoulder and ran his thumb gingerly over a spot where the fabric was beginning to pill. It was the first time he'd touched her since waking her that morning with such a languid, thorough kiss, and a warm shudder wound through her at the simple contact. For a long moment, Roxy watched the slow, casual caress of his thumb as it stroked across her shoulder, her heartbeat quickening as he gradually increased the pressure.

With each touch, she could feel the heat of his hand penetrating the thick wool, and all she could do was remember when he had made the same rhythmic, circular motions with his thumb on another part of her body. She sucked in a quick, quiet breath at the memory, feeling her face—and that other body part—growing warm. At the small sound, Spencer lifted his gaze and saw her watching the movement of his thumb, and she knew immediately that he was recalling exactly what she was recalling. Finally, he stopped, then let his fingers skim down the length of her arm before covering her hand with his.

"Back to what?" he asked innocently, as if that last caress had never occurred.

"Back to you trying to show me how much we have in

common.'' Her voice came out sounding low and husky, and she cleared her throat indelicately.

"And your point is...?''

Roxy shook her head. "It's not going to work. Just because a few sparks fly between us when we get close, that doesn't mean anything. Physical attraction doesn't last long. I still say we're way too far apart socially for anything between us to ever be more than temporary.''

"Roxy...''

She stood and made her way quickly to his desk, then spun around to face him. "Forget about it, Spencer. Forget about us. It won't work.''

He eyed her thoughtfully, then glanced down at his watch. "It's almost quitting time, and I have a meeting after work that I—that *we*—need to attend. Business. After that, we can finish the evening at one of my favorite places.''

She rolled her eyes. "Great. I can only imagine how much fun *that's* going to be.''

"You'll like it. I promise.''

"Uh-huh. Sure. Okay. Whatever.''

"Whatever,'' he repeated with a smile she wasn't sure she liked. But he said nothing further to elaborate. Instead, he stood confidently and made his way to the door.

Roxy, too, tossed the word around in her head for a moment, then decided that *whatever* must be the most understated word in the English language. It could mean anything. It could mean everything.

Or, she thought with a sigh as she stood to follow him out of the room, it could mean nothing at all.

Eleven

The "meeting" that Spencer had to attend actually wound up being a cocktail party in a posh Ballston high-rise. Roxy felt more than a little out of place dressed in her blue jeans and aged, stretched-out sweater, and she silently berated Spencer for not having warned her to wear something more appropriate.

Not that she owned any party clothes that had a hope in hell of competing with the glad rags rich folks wore, she reminded herself. But a number of the people present had obviously come straight from work and still had on the uniform of big business, and she probably could have held her own, fashion-wise, anyway, with most of them. But Roxy was a practical woman. She didn't dress for work unless she was going to be working. And at the moment, she was wishing…

Oh, hell, she thought with a sigh. It didn't matter what she was wishing right now. She had been wishing for so many things lately, the wish fairies were going to turn their backs on her for good. Especially since all of those wishes had been the kind that were impossible to grant. She ought to try focusing on reality for a change, she told herself. Maybe then she would stop dreaming her days away and be able to actually accomplish something.

Like finding Spencer's sister, for example. Now *that* was something that was going to occupy her time. Just how was she supposed to go about searching for a person when she knew nothing about that person beyond a name that appeared on a birth certificate that wasn't even valid anymore? Charlotte McCormick could be anyone by now. And she could be anywhere. Even though Roxy knew the exact time and place of the woman's birth, she was clueless as to her whereabouts now.

There was a very good chance that Charlotte had remained in the area, she reminded herself. Although Washington, D.C., was an incredibly transient place, the people born here had a tendency to stay here. Unfortunately, *here* involved a total area consisting of two states, a half-dozen counties, scores of communities and one of the most densely populated cities in the country. Even if Charlotte had remained here—and that was a big *if*—it could take months, maybe years, to find her.

Not for the first time since taking Spencer's case, Roxy wished Bingo were still alive. He'd know what to do. He'd find Charlotte McCormick in no time. Her grandfather had been amazing when it came to locating people, part bloodhound, part computer data bank, part psychic.

She wished he were still alive for other reasons, too. Over the past few weeks—ever since laying eyes on Spencer Melbourne—Roxy had felt the need to talk to someone, both about the case and about life. And Bingo had been the only person alive who had ever seemed to understand her. Most people had considered her grandfather to be a rough, uneducated, impatient man. And, in many ways, Roxy knew he had been. But he'd been a loving, compassionate, decent man, too, in his own way. At least where his only granddaughter had been concerned.

Yeah, Bingo Matheny had been able to coldcock a man in a barroom brawl with a single blow to the chin. But he'd also been known to fire up the heating pad and brew chamomile tea on those occasions when Roxy had come home from school with cramps. He'd been matter-of-fact about everything in life, from pool hustlers to an adolescent's moody reproductive system.

Bingo had just been a good guy. The only good guy Roxy had ever known, the only person who had ever told her he loved her. And even though his words of affection had always been punctuated with a good, solid punch to her upper arm, she'd known he was telling her the truth. Bingo had loved her. And she had loved him. She wished she could have him back, even for five minutes. So that she could ask him to set her on the right course where Spencer's case was concerned. So that, even for five minutes, she wouldn't have to feel so all alone.

"You okay, Roxy?"

For one brief, hopeful moment, she thought it was Bingo's voice speaking to her from beyond the pale, and the comfort that had always come with his presence surrounded her like an aged, much-loved quilt. Then, too quickly, she realized it was Spencer, not her grandfather, who stood beside her. In spite of that, for some reason she would never be able to fathom, the same warm, wistful sense of companionship and being watched out for that she'd always felt with Bingo stayed with her.

Without giving the sensation further consideration, Roxy shook the feeling off. There was no way Spencer Melbourne could ever step in and take Bingo's place. No way would he ever be able to love her or understand her or comfort her the way her grandfather had. He just wasn't that kind of guy.

"Yeah, I'm okay," she told him. "Why?"

He hesitated a moment before telling her, "You looked a little lonely over here by yourself."

She shook her head, but not to negate his remark. She was feeling lonely. But there was no reason Spencer had to know that. "I've been thinking about someone."

"So have I."

She ignored the implicit meaning behind his words and

clarified, "Bingo. I was thinking about my grandfather. About how much I miss him."

"Oh."

Yeah, she thought, Bingo Matheny's instincts had been right on the mark about people, every single time. Where they were coming from, where they were going, where they wanted to be. And although Roxy seemed to have inherited a great deal from her paternal grandfather, she'd had no such luck where her own instincts were concerned.

Case in point—Spencer Melbourne. In spite of knowing what kind of man he was, she hadn't been able to keep herself from falling for him. Hard. And although she was a profound believer in history repeating itself—especially history that's been long forgotten—she was helpless to stop her roller-coaster emotions from taking her heart on a wild ride.

She pushed her confusing thoughts aside and backtracked in her contemplations instead. "I was thinking that Bingo would have known what to do about Charlotte," she told Spencer. "He'd know where to start looking for her. Me, I don't have a clue."

"I have faith in you."

She expelled a dubious chuckle of mirth. "Well, that makes one of us."

She felt his hands on her shoulders and, for the first time since entering the party, looked up and gave him her full attention. She could almost let herself believe that the look in his eyes was an honest, heartfelt affection for her. She could almost convince herself that the sense of well-being she'd just experienced had happened for a good reason. She could almost allow herself to be drawn into whatever Spencer Melbourne was offering.

Almost.

But something prevented her from taking that final step. Instead, she dropped her gaze back down to the drink she held in her hand, the one she'd been nursing since someone pressed it into her grasp nearly the moment they'd arrived. It was diluted and limp looking, the ice melted down to almost nothing. When she sipped it, it lacked flavor and character and zing. For some reason, she identified greatly with that drink.

"We'll find Charlotte," Spencer assured her.

"We?" she repeated. "I thought that was my job."

"It used to be your job. Now it's *our* quest."

She sipped her drink again and let her gaze rove around the room, lighting on anything that wasn't Spencer Melbourne. "Speak for yourself. This isn't a quest for me. I'm only doing it because you're writing me checks."

"You care as much about finding my sister as I do," he countered. "And not just because of the money you're going to earn. You care, Roxy." He curled his index finger under her chin and tilted her head so that she was looking up at him again. "You *care*."

She rolled her shoulders in what she hoped was an idle shrug and turned her head so that his hand was clutching air. "It's just another case to me."

He dropped that hand to his side, squeezed her shoulder with the other and told her, "You'll never convince me of that."

She shrugged again, hoping her phony nonchalance looked more convincing than it felt. "Suit yourself."

"Okay."

She glanced up to see what he meant by his short, sudden agreement, only to have him curl his fingers around her forearm and tug her gently along behind him. Before she could stop him, he was calling out his farewell to the host and uttering hasty goodbyes to a few others. Then, without ceremony, he hauled Roxy through the front door.

Within minutes, they were in the building's parking garage, and Spencer was opening the passenger door for her, stopping just shy of stuffing her into the car. Somehow, Roxy managed to do that herself, then waited while he circled the back of the car, unlocked his own door and climbed inside. Instead of starting up the engine, however, he reached over the console between the two seats and pulled her into his arms.

"What are you doing?" she said with a surprised gasp.

"You told me to suit myself," he reminded her. "And it

suits me to neck in the car with you. Ever since last night, I've finally pinned down what it is about you that's been making me feel so crazy.''

She knew it wasn't a good idea to ask for clarification, but found herself saying, anyway, ''Oh? And what's that?''

With a soft smile, he twined a length of her hair around one finger and said, ''You make me feel like a kid again, Roxy. You make me want to do things I haven't done for years. Things I've never done before.'' He glanced wistfully behind his seat into the darkness behind them. ''I just wish I still had the old Mustang I used to drive. It had a much bigger back seat than this. Well, not much bigger, but...big enough.''

Roxy, too, glanced over her shoulder into the tiny storage compartment the manufacturer had installed into the rented sports car instead of a back seat.

''Big enough for what?'' she asked a little breathlessly.

He smiled. ''Oh, I think you know.''

''I have no idea what you're talking about,'' she lied. ''Something about back seats, was it?'' She looked over her shoulder again. ''Or maybe the lack thereof?''

His smile faltered some, and his gaze dropped to her mouth. ''What I was talking about,'' he said softly, ''was that there was a time in my life when there was nothing to obstruct some serious window fogging. As it is, this—'' he thumped the plastic console between them ''—is going to make what I want to do a challenge.'' He smiled once more, and this time the expression was positively salacious. ''Then again, there are other obstacles to overcome that will be infinitely more challenging. Not that I'm not up to those, either,'' he added quietly.

Before Roxy could object to whatever he had planned, he kissed her, and then she suddenly didn't want to object at all. What she wanted was to melt into that kiss and go limp all over while Spencer dragged his mouth along every inch of her body. What she wanted was for the moment to never ever end.

And for the longest time, it didn't. His lips on hers were

warm and willing, his tongue teasing and tempestuous. He
cupped her jaw in his hand, then traced his fingers down her
throat and over her shoulder before tenting his fingers over
her breast. Even through the heavy fabric of her sweater, he
found her nipple, rolling it under the pad of his thumb until
she thought she would go mad.

Helpless to respond, she knifed her fingers through his hair,
skimming his gruff jaw with her palm along the way. He was
rough where she was soft, blunt where she was curved. And
suddenly, for some reason, their differences compelled more
than bothered her.

"Why do you do this to me?" she gasped, wondering how
her willpower could flee so readily every time Spencer came
anywhere near her.

He chuckled low against her mouth. "Why not?"

"Because it's crazy, that's why."

He moved his mouth to her chin, her jaw, her cheek. "It's
not crazy," he whispered. "It's what we do to each other.
How we respond to each other. It's perfectly natural."

Automatically, she tilted her head to the side, giving him
freer access to the tender flesh of her nape. "No, this isn't
natural. This is…"

"What?"

He nipped lightly at her jaw, then nibbled her earlobe before drawing the tip of his tongue slowly down her neck to
taste the pulse raging wildly just beneath her skin. Roxy
groaned with wanting, holding his head resolutely against her,
knowing she should release him and push him away, terrified
of dying from unsatisfied need if she did.

"It's so…so primitive," she sputtered. "So basic…"

"Like I said, natural."

"It feels unnatural," she objected. "Like nothing the gods
ever intended. It isn't right, Spencer. We shouldn't."

"It's more than right. Trust me, Roxy," he said softly,
nipping her earlobe again. "I'll take care of you. You know
I will."

*C'mon, Roxy, trust me. You know I'll take care of you. I
always have, haven't I?*

A massive wave of déjà vu washed over her when he uttered his promise, and she realized she'd heard the same words spoken in the same way so many years ago. It suddenly occurred to her that what was happening now had happened before. But what she recalled wasn't her last tryst with Spencer.

The memories that crowded into her head now involved another blue-blooded, aristocratic, much-monied guy who had been way out of her league. Spencer's words echoed the ones spoken that night when her adolescent innocence was overrun by Reggie Dodds, and without warning, Roxy became that same frightened sixteen-year-old girl who had misplaced both her trust and her heart.

Spencer was so much like Reggie, she realized with a start, tearing her mouth free of his. She wondered how she could have forgotten so easily. As she studied him in the dim light that barely permeated the car's interior, she could almost swear it was Reggie, and not Spencer, sitting in the driver's seat, his breathing ragged, his face damp, his voice full of promises and cajoling. Same coloring, same background, same clothes, same words. The car they were sitting in was a lot like the one Reggie had driven, identical in color, size and price range. Even the smell of the leather upholstery was familiar. It had been a car like this where Roxy had been robbed of so many things—her virginity, her innocence, her soul.

"Roxy?"

Her name cut through the shadows that haunted the car's interior, and for one wild moment, she wasn't sure who had said it. Spencer, she reminded herself. It had to be Spencer. She hadn't seen Reggie for nearly fifteen years. And she would be more than a fool to wind up in a situation like that with a man like him again.

"Roxy? What is it? What's wrong?"

Instead of answering, she only shook her head mutely and tried to push him away. But Spencer clung to her, gripped her arms even more fiercely than before and tried to pull her back to him again.

"No!" she cried, more vehemently than was necessary.

Immediately, he released her, raising his hands, palms out, to shoulder level. Whether it was a gesture of surrender or a show of good faith, Roxy wasn't sure. But Spencer sat there staring at her for some moments before either of them spoke again.

Gradually, he lowered his hands and dipped his head toward her, as if trying to decipher her expression in the dim lights of the garage. "You want to tell me what the hell's going on?"

"Take me home."

It was all she could think of to say. It was what she had said to Reggie that night so long ago, and somehow the words seemed appropriate.

And just as Reggie had that night, Spencer shook his head no. "We're not going anywhere until you tell me what's wrong."

"Take me home," she repeated.

"Not until you're straight with me."

"Spencer, please…"

Her voice broke then, and she couldn't finish what she had tried to say. Instead, she lifted a shaky hand to cover her eyes and willed herself not to cry. She hadn't cried that night, nor on any of the nights that had followed. She'd actually managed to convince herself back then that what she was doing was the right thing to do, because she'd loved Reggie, she'd respected Reggie, she'd trusted Reggie. He'd promised to take care of her. He'd promised to make her happy. He might as well have promised her the moon.

"Who was it?"

Spencer's words cut through the darkness, barely piercing the mind-numbing memories that had seeped into Roxy's brain. "Who was who?" she asked quietly.

"Who was the son of a bitch that made you so damned wary?"

She sighed, bunching a fistful of hair in her hand before raking her fingers through the unruly mass. It was pointless to deny what he was suggesting. Reggie had been a son of a bitch, and he'd done something that had indeed made her damned wary. Actually, these days, Roxy preferred to consider what Reggie did to her as more along the lines of teaching her a lesson about life. A lesson about chemistry, even. Don't mix blue blood with blue-collar. Because what you'll wind up with is a mess.

Surrendering to Spencer's inquisition, she inhaled a deep, fortifying breath and, as she released it, said, "His name was Reginald Bleeker Dodds III." She turned to look at him, knowing the intensity of her gaze would be lost in the darkness. "Feel better now?"

Spencer's eyebrows shot up in surprise, as if he hadn't expected her to actually name someone in response to his question. "Not yet," he told her. "But we'll get to that."

Roxy shook her head slightly, then rested it in her hand and propped her elbow on the car's dashboard. "Oh, I just bet we will."

Spencer was clearly unimpressed with her casual posture. "You're damned right we will. But first, I think the least you could do is fill me in on the details about this guy."

"Why?"

"Because I think I have a right to know."

"Why?"

He expelled an exasperated sound and extended his hand toward her. But instead of taking it, she only stared at it, pretending she had no idea why he was even offering the gesture. His eyes darkened angrily at her unwillingness to accommodate him, and he dropped his hand back to the console in a loose fist.

"Because I care about you, Roxy, that's why. If you've been hurt, I want to know about it."

She emitted a single, humorless chuckle. "What's the point, Spencer? Why drag up something that happened more than fifteen years ago?"

"Because it's keeping you from being happy now, that's the point."

Her voice went flat as she told him, "Reggie is history.

What he did or didn't do does *not* keep me from being happy now.''

"Then you won't mind talking about it, will you?"

"It won't change anything."

He hesitated a moment, and she thought he might drop it. She should have known better.

"How do you know?" he asked her.

She turned away from his penetrating gaze to stare out the windshield at the dark parking garage instead. "I just do."

"Humor me."

"At my own expense? No, thanks."

"Roxy..."

"What?"

"Tell me what happened."

Her patience at an end, she turned again, enough to fix her gaze on his, and snapped, "I got screwed by some wealthy, socially upstanding guy in the only two ways that count, all right? Get the picture, rich boy? Satisfied now?"

He eyed her back and said, "What, you got dumped? You got dumped by some jerk who just happened to be wealthy, so now you've declared the entire male half of the upper-income-level spectrum unworthy? Hell, Roxy, everybody gets dumped, rich or not, including me. Get over it already."

Her lips thinned, and she frowned at him. "There was more to it than that."

"Well, here's your chance to tell me all about it."

"Fine." She swiveled in her seat again and reached for the seat belt, clicking it resolutely into place. "You want the long version, you got it. Take me back to my place and I'll fix us a couple of drinks and fill you in on the whole sordid story." As he ground the engine to life, she muttered, "You're gonna love this one, Spencer. It's right up your alley."

"I said take me back to my place, not yours."

Spencer remained silent as he met Roxy's gaze, killed the car's engine, turned off the headlights and unfastened his seat belt.

"Spencer?"

Still watching her, he opened the car door and got out, then slammed it shut behind him and circled the front of the car, all the while focusing his gaze intently on hers through the windshield. When he reached the passenger side, he unlatched the door and held it open, waiting for her to join him on the sidewalk in front of his house.

"I'm not getting out," she announced. "I told you to take me home."

"You seem to have forgotten that we're still celebrating a day in *my* life," he reminded her. "The twenty-four hours aren't up yet. You owe me a night."

She shook her head in disbelief, but continued to stare forward through the windshield instead of at him. "Man, you have got some nerve. In case you've forgotten, you've already had a night with me."

He chuckled low. "Oh, believe me, it's unlikely I'll ever forget that night. But that night happened before you owed me one. That night was one you gave freely."

"Says who?"

"You sure as hell didn't put up much of a fight."

Even in the pale light of the street lamp overhead, he could see that his remark hit its target perfectly. Her cheeks flamed pink and her eyes narrowed. But she still refused to look at him.

"On the contrary," he added, hoping to raise a spark of life in her, "if memory serves, you were all over me that night."

His comment had the desired effect. With an unprecedented *snap*, her seat belt flew back into its casing, and Roxy was out of the car like a shot. She stood toe-to-toe with him, her head thrown back in defiance, her fists curled loosely at her sides, waiting to see if he would dare say something more, ready to belt him when he did.

"And tonight," he concluded, deciding he might as well go for broke, "I plan to be all over you."

Her fists tightened. "You can try it, pal," she muttered. "And see what it gets you."

"Promises, promises," he murmured softly.

"Yeah, I bet *you're* good with those, too."

He wasn't sure why she'd emphasized her statement the way she had, but he figured he'd get to the bottom of it soon enough. So he angled his body toward his house and swept his arm in the general direction of his front door.

"Coming?" he asked her, hoping his voice didn't sound as sarcastic to her as it did to him. Her lack of response was making him angrier by the minute. By now, she should have at least *tried* to hit him. The fact that she was being so docile didn't sit well with Spencer at all.

Without further comment, she pushed past him, remaining silent while he unlocked and opened the front door. She was quiet, too, when they entered, making her way wordlessly to the living room, where she spun around at its center and glared at him. Spencer glared back as he closed the door behind them and sauntered leisurely into the room.

"Drink?" he asked in much the way he had the first time she'd stood in the same spot.

Her expression now was nothing like it had been then, however. That day, she'd looked considerably less malevolent, considerably less likely to throttle him with her bare hands. Her verbal response now was different, too. "Scotch if you have it," she told him. "Neat."

He smiled at her, though not because he was particularly happy at the moment. "What do you know? That's what I prefer, too. Gee, we really do have so much in common."

Her gaze was piercing as she snapped, "Why do you keep harping on that?"

"Who's harping?" he countered as he went to fix their drinks. "We do have a lot in common."

"We have nothing in common."

He grinned as he poured their Scotch. "How did you vote in the last presidential election?"

"Democrat," she responded immediately, thrusting her chin up defiantly, clearly expecting him to reply in the opposite.

Instead, he told her honestly, "So did I. What kind of movies do you like best?"

Her conviction seeming to have deflated some, her posture did, too. Still, she seemed a bit defensive as she answered, "Action-adventure."

"Same here. What kind of music do you listen to at night before you go to bed?"

She glanced down at the floor. "Jazz."

"Cool or hot?"

She made a restless sound before looking up at him again and confessing, "Cool."

He wiggled his eyebrows at her, letting her know she'd replied to the question exactly as he would have himself. Then he continued, "I bet you're a mystery buff, too."

She nodded slowly, and he could see that the gesture came to her reluctantly.

"Let me guess. Patricia Cornwell, Tony Hillerman and Scott Turow."

An exasperated sigh told him he'd hit her preferences right on the mark. "And Taylor McCafferty, too," she said. "I like her stuff a lot."

"I'll have to check her out."

"You do that." Her voice dripped with sarcasm, and before he could ask her anything more, she told him, "But little facts like that mean nothing. It's our life-style differences that matter, anyway."

He gazed at her, dumbfounded. "You don't see the similarities in our two life-styles?"

She made a sour face at him. "Of course not. Because there are no similarities in our life-styles."

He recapped the Scotch and made his way toward her with two crystal tumblers, pressing one into her hand before consuming a generous mouthful of the other. "Think back, Roxy. I spent a day in your life and you spent a day in mine, and neither day was all that different from the other."

She gaped at him incredulously. "What are you, blind? Those two days were totally different."

"Consider these facts." His expression intent, he held up a clenched fist for her inspection, then deliberately unfolded his index finger. "Number one. We both conceded we normally hurry through a prefab breakfast, but because of the presence of each other in our days, we did something a little special.''

She started to object, but he cut her off by lifting a second finger to join the first.

''Number two,'' he continued. ''We both wound up making ourselves late and having to make a run for it.'' A third finger joined the first two. ''Number three. We both had to spend part of our day listening to the ravings of a lunatic, and we both had to pretend we took him seriously.''

''Oh, come on, Spencer. That's—''

''Number four,'' he continued relentlessly, still counting off his points on his digits. ''On both days, we ended up parked in a rented car breathing heavily down each other's shirts and fogging up the glass, only to be rudely interrupted before we could...accomplish our intentions. On your day, it was a security guard. On my day, it was Reginald Bleeker Dodds III.''

She had the decency not to comment on that, he noted. Not verbally, anyway. But her cheeks flamed red and her pupils expanded enough to nearly eclipse the dark brown of her irises.

''Number five,'' he went on, dropping his voice just a fraction. He flexed his last finger, holding all five up for her inspection, then cupped her jaw gently in his hand. ''Number five,'' he concluded softly, ''we ended the day wanting each other more than anything in the world, but doing nothing about it.''

She hesitated a moment, then swallowed with some difficulty. ''You're reaching, Spencer,'' she finally said. But her voice was low and thready when she spoke. Clearly, she wasn't as confident of her words as she wanted to be.

''Yeah?'' he asked impatiently. ''Well, maybe I am. But why the hell can't you at least try to meet me halfway?''

She said nothing in response, only continued to gaze at him with those huge, hungry eyes that made him hurt all over. *Dammit*, what was her problem? he wondered. Why couldn't she just give him a chance? What was holding her back? Why

did she refuse to give even an inch where their relationship—
or at least their *potential* relationship—was concerned?

As if she could read his mind, her eyes softened some, and
her body seemed to relax. When she lifted her drink to her
lips, he could see that her hand was still shaking. The tremble
seemed to overcome her whole body then, and she wrapped
her arms fiercely around her midsection, as if trying to warm
herself.

"Are you cold?" he asked her.

She shook her head. "Not in any way that can be
warmed."

He lifted a hand to her hair, skimming his fingers gently
over the dark tresses before dropping it helplessly back to his
side. "Tell me what happened, Roxy."

When her eyes met his again, they were different somehow,
almost the eyes of a stranger. She seemed younger suddenly,
more vulnerable. Gone was the confident, self-assured woman
he'd come to admire so much. In her place was someone who
seemed confused, uncertain, haunted.

"Okay," she finally relented. "I'll tell you. And then I'm
going home. I'll find your sister for your, Spencer. Because
I'm a private investigator, and that's what you've hired me
to do. But after tonight, that's all I'll be for you."

He didn't like the finality of her words, didn't like the fact
that she seemed to be telling him she refused to be anything
for anybody other than what she was for herself. It was an
odd assertion to make. Why would he want her to be anything
other than what she was?

Instead of asking her, he just nodded silently. They'd talk,
he told himself. And then he'd decide what to do.

Twelve

"Reggie was a rich kid," she started, her voice sounding almost mechanical as she spoke. "Handsome, charming, sexy. Like you," she added, meeting his gaze fleetingly before darting it away again. "He even looked like you. Same coloring, same size. A lot younger, of course, but stand the two of you next to each other fifteen years ago, you probably could have passed for brothers."

"And that's what bothers you? That I resemble an old boyfriend?"

She shook her head. "No. Of course not. Not the part about looks, anyway."

"So what is it, then?"

She sighed heavily and moved away from him, taking several measured strides toward the windows that looked out onto the street in front of his house. With her back to him, he was denied her facial expressions, and that bothered him. But her posture told him she wouldn't welcome his nearness right now. So he forced himself to stay put, and watched her from a distance instead.

"Reggie was like you in other ways, too. He liked flashy, expensive cars, had a lot of charisma, came from old money, was planning on taking over his father's position as chairman of the board someday."

Spencer shrugged. "And?"

He saw her shoulders rise and fall, but didn't hear the sigh the gesture indicated. "And...he did some things to me he shouldn't have."

Spencer's heart stopped beating for a moment, and heat flared up in parts of his body he hadn't known he could feel. "Like what?"

Roxy turned around then, and he could see that she was still the frightened woman he'd glimpsed only moments ago. "He was my first," she said. "My first...you know."

"He took your virginity," Spencer supplied, wondering why she felt awkward about saying it herself.

"Among other things, yeah." Her voice seemed hollow somehow, nothing at all like he was used to hearing it.

"What other things?" he asked.

She seemed hesitant to continue, and when she finally did, she sounded distant and cool, as if she were speaking about someone other than herself. "It started that night. The first time we..."

Again her voice trailed off, as if she were reluctant to say any more. Finally, she cleared her throat and began again. "The first time we, um, did it, we were parked in his car. The same way you and I were parked tonight. Sitting in that car with you..."

Her voice trailed off again, and again he got the feeling that she was remembering something she really didn't want to remember.

"When it happened with Reggie," she began again, "I really wasn't ready for it. I hadn't known him all that long, and I didn't want to take that big a step yet. But we'd been necking for a while, and...well...you know how it is with teenagers."

"Refresh my memory." Spencer bit the words out angrily, already certain he knew what was coming next.

"They, um, they get a little bit out of control sometimes. Reggie said, 'Trust me, Roxy. I'll take care of you.' And even though I told him I did trust him, I just wasn't ready and I didn't want to do it, he shoved himself inside me. And it hurt like hell."

There was so much more that she wasn't saying. Spencer could see it in her eyes. She'd felt violated and betrayed. The son of a bitch really had done a number on her.

"I think they call that date rape now," he said, amazed that he could keep his voice so level.

"Yeah, well, back then they weren't quite so charitable. Back then they pretty much just thought of it as some girl getting what she was asking for. And, hey, at least it was with a nice guy, right? At least he was cute and rich and said he'd take care of me, right? What did I have to complain about? A lot of girls would have been dying to drop their drawers for Reggie."

"But you weren't one of them."

She sighed again, jamming her fingers into her hair, then paced restlessly to the other side of the room. But she was no closer to Spencer now than she had been before, and he could still sense her need for distance. So even though instinct told him to go over and gather her into his arms, he didn't. He already reminded her of someone who hadn't taken no for an answer. He didn't want her to think he would just as easily disregard her wants himself.

"I think..." she went on hesitantly. "I think eventually I would have let Reggie be the one. That's what made it so difficult. I just wasn't ready that night. I didn't want it that night. I was afraid." She met Spencer's gaze briefly again, then glanced back down at her drink. "But Reggie did it, anyway."

This time Spencer was the one to sigh, but his was an attempt to quell the rage and repugnance he felt building inside himself. He wasn't surprised by what she'd revealed. Unfortunately, what Roxy described probably happened a lot. And he didn't doubt that the experience had influenced her greatly since then. He just didn't know what the hell to do or say to counteract the effects.

"Even that's not the worst of it, though," she went on.

When he looked at her, she was still staring down into her glass, still avoiding his gaze, and he could feel her slipping further into a place he knew she'd rather not visit. He told himself he should bring her back, should do whatever he had to do to shelter her from the pain and anguish that filled her past. But Roxy Matheny wasn't a woman who demanded coddling. At least, the Roxy Matheny he'd come to know wasn't. This new version was unfamiliar to him. He had no idea how to react to her now.

"I didn't leave him after that night," she said. "I stayed with him. Even though what happened was...horrible...I thought that was the way it was supposed to be. I just... Reggie had always said he'd take care of me. And that's what I thought he was doing. But, of course, he didn't take care of me at all. Things just got worse."

"What do you mean?" Spencer had to force the question out, certain he didn't want to hear the gory details, still needing to know, however, whether or not she had come to terms with what had happened to her.

"It was just a bad relationship, Spencer, okay? Can't we leave it at that?"

"No. We can't. I can't. And I don't think you can, either. That's part of the problem, Roxy."

She looked up at the ceiling, and only then did he see the moisture shining in her eyes. She was trying not to cry. And failing miserably.

"He, um..." She sniffled before raising a hand to cover her eyes. "He was kind of a control freak. He needed to know what I was doing all the time, demanded to know who I was with, had to talk to me every night. And every time he saw me—which was nearly every day—he had to make love to me. In his own...unique...way."

She spun around then, turning her back to him once more. "And I put up with it. I let him get away with it. Because in some twisted, perverted way, I thought I loved him. And I thought he loved me. Instead, all I did was turn myself over to him. I lost myself completely. I just...I don't know how it happened, but it did."

"How long?" The two words were all Spencer could manage.

"How long did I stay with him?" she asked.

"Yes."

"A little over a year."

Spencer inhaled a silent breath and held it, willing his violent heartbeat to steady. "More than a year," he repeated.

He saw her nod.

"How did it finally end?"

She laughed, the sound grotesque and surreal and in no way jovial. "That's the best part," she said. "I didn't leave him. He left me. In a manner of speaking. One day, he told me out of the blue that he was engaged to be married to the daughter of a family friend. He said he thought it would be a good idea to cool our relationship while the wedding plans were under way, but that he'd call me as soon as he got back from his honeymoon, and we could pick up where we left off."

Finally, Roxy turned around and faced Spencer again. He studied her closely and thought he saw a hint of the fire that he knew was so inherent in Roxy Matheny flickering back to life in her eyes.

"Isn't that a hoot?" she asked bitterly. "If it hadn't been for that, I might still be with him. I might be one of those poor, pathetic women you hear about, in love with their abusers because they just don't know how to live life any other way, because they don't have enough faith in themselves to strike out on their own."

Spencer doubted that. But instead of countering her vision of her own future, he asked, "Where was Bingo during all this?"

"Bingo was around. He hated Reggie. On more than one occasion, he threatened to beat the hell out of him, and I think he would have if he hadn't worried that doing it would alienate me. Reggie almost came between me and my grandfather.

But Bingo figured I was a big girl and could take care of myself. I thought so, too. Obviously we were both wrong.''

Spencer and Roxy remained silent, simply gazing at each other from opposite sides of the room. He wanted to go to her, wanted to take her in his arms and tell her that all that was in the past, and that everything would be all right now. But he knew it was a little more complicated than that. Youthful experiences ran deep in the soul. Whether good or bad, what happened to people when they were children and adolescents tended to mark them for life.

Hell, he should know.

"So did Reggie call you when he got back from his honeymoon?'' he finally asked.

Roxy's gaze fell back to her drink. "I don't know. I moved out of the apartment I'd been sharing with another girl—I'd moved out of Bingo's place because of his objections to Reggie—and back in with Bingo. If Reggie ever called, Bingo probably threatened to kill him if he ever came near me. And although Reggie was a lot of things, stupid wasn't one of them. He never would have messed with Bingo.''

"So then, really, you left Reggie.''

Her head snapped up at that, her eyes glistening and dark when they met his. "What?''

"You left Reggie. He didn't leave you.''

"No, he did leave me. I never would have had the strength to leave him.''

"Yes, you did. If you hadn't had the strength, you would have waited for him to come back from his honeymoon, and you would have kept letting him beat you up emotionally. As it was, you got out and turned your life around.''

She shook her head vaguely, but her expression was clearly confused. "No, I...''

"Roxy,'' he began, still not certain what else he was going to say.

"Reggie owned me, Spencer,'' she interrupted him, as if he hadn't spoken his last observations at all. "Body, heart and soul, he *owned* me for more than a year.'' She paused for a moment, then told him, "When I'm with you, I feel myself slipping into that again. I feel myself losing part of myself to you. Tonight, you said I make you feel like a kid again. Well, unfortunately, that's what happens to me when I'm with you, too. Only I don't *want* to feel that way, ever again. I can't let that happen. I just can't. I couldn't survive it a second time.''

"Roxy, you won't have to. What happened then is nothing like what's happening between us now. Don't you see?''

She shook her head. "All I see is me feeling the same way I did back then. I think about you constantly, I feel completely in tune to you whenever we're together. I feel you *inside* me, Spencer. I feel myself giving up parts of myself to you. And I can't surrender myself again. Not to you or anyone.''

"I'm not asking for your surrender.''

"Aren't you?''

"Of course not. What you feel about me, Roxy…it's exactly the same way I feel about you. This isn't about possession, it's about caring. It's about falling in love.''

"No.'' The one-word reply was adamant. "It's not love. That's what Reggie called it, too, but that's not what it is.''

Spencer nodded. "You're right about that, at least. What Reggie did to you had nothing to do with love.''

He took a few steps toward her, then stopped when she started to edge backward herself, swearing under his breath at the man who had made her so skittish. If he ever crossed paths with one Reginald Bleeker Dodds III, he'd make sure there would never be a IV.

He pushed the thought away and focused on Roxy instead. "Let me show you what love is, Roxy. Give me one more chance. Then, if you still feel like you're losing yourself, if you still think I want more to possess you than to love you, you can leave, and I promise I'll never bother you again.''

She remained silent, and only gazed at him with those huge, hungry eyes. He took another experimental step forward, heartened some when she made no move to flee. Slowly, little by little, he closed the distance between them until he stood directly before her. Her eyes were still damp, her nose a little red, her lips fuller and sexier than he ever recalled them being. Briefly, he cupped her cheek in his palm, then shifted his hand to skim his fingertips gingerly over her mouth. She parted her lips a fraction, and her warm breath kissed his fingers. He touched his index finger to her chin, then leaned forward and covered her mouth with his.

He took his time as he kissed her, sensing that it was best not to rush things just yet. He touched her cheek lightly with his fingertips, ran the backs of his knuckles along her jaw and under her chin until he could cup the smooth column of her throat in his hand. Her pulse raged wildly beneath his thumb, her heart pumping double-time in response to his touch. His own heartbeat quickened at the knowledge that he so aroused her, and he forced himself not to pick up the pace.

Slow. He wanted to go slow with Roxy. She was skittish and wary, and he had to prove to her that her fears where he was concerned were completely unfounded. He wasn't going to use or betray her. He wasn't going to hurt her. He had to make her realize that. And the only way he knew how was to take his time and show her just how much she meant to him.

"I love you, Roxy," he told her softly, covering her mouth quickly again to prevent her from denouncing his vow.

His tongue darted lightly over her lips before dancing past them, and he tasted her delicately, flicking the tip of his tongue against hers, before sucking her lower lip between his teeth for an idle nibble. She gasped at the intimacy, then her body seemed to relax some. Spencer moved his hand to the back of her neck, cradling her nape in his palm, tilting her head back to facilitate a more thorough exploration of her mouth. He suckled her lip for a moment longer, then dipped his tongue back inside her mouth, this time savoring her more fully.

The hand Roxy had clenched in his shirt slowly began to ease, her fingers releasing the fabric to splay open over his cheek instead. She threaded her fingers into his hair, to the back of his head, curling around his nape to pull his mouth closer to hers.

When he sensed her capitulation, he moved his hand to her

hip, dragging his fingers down along her thigh. Roxy's eyelids fluttered closed, and her lips parted in anticipation. Not wanting to disappoint her, Spencer skimmed his hand back up again, curving his palm over her fanny, rubbing her behind with deft maneuvers, pressing her belly to the apex of his thighs. They groaned in unison as he swelled against her, both their bodies shifting automatically to make the most of the situation.

His other hand traveled up along her torso, fingering each rib until he reached the lower curve of her breast. Without hesitating, he covered the soft mound with his hand, fingers stiff, palm flat, mimicking the same circles his other hand still drew on her derriere.

Roxy went stock-still, one hand remaining tangled in his hair, one fiercely gripping his upper arm. But her eyes closed completely, and he could see that she was succumbing to the pressure he exerted. So, smiling, Spencer decided to…increase the pressure. So to speak.

He dropped his hands to the hem of her sweater and pulled it up over her head. She seemed startled at first, but when he quickly returned to his previous position—one hand cupping her fanny, the other covering her breast—she immediately fell back to her languid pose. He smiled again, moving closer, rubbing himself against her, the press of his hard shaft growing larger between them making them both go a little crazy.

He continued to draw idle circles on her breast, gradually narrowing his focus until the pad of his thumb rested on her nipple, moving the tight bud back and forth, up and down. And when he could no longer tolerate the look of expectant anguish on her face, he lowered his head and sucked the lace-covered peak into his mouth, laving it with the flat of his tongue before tickling it with the tip.

Roxy's fingers convulsed in his hair, but instead of trying to push him away, she held him still against her bosom, silently begging him to continue. For long moments, Spencer suckled her through her brassiere, the frail fabric growing wet beneath his ministrations. Finally, he reached behind her and unhooked the garment, then pulled it slowly down her arms to discard it on the floor. Her breast was wet and shiny from the attention his mouth had paid it, and the full, pink flesh beckoned to his mouth again. This time when he responded to the summons, it was more fiercely, more insistently, more recklessly.

This time, feeling himself slipping beyond the boundaries of control, he nipped the dark aureola lightly with his teeth, kissing the violated spot gently when Roxy sucked in her breath. He was about to apologize for his transgression, but she softly—so softly he almost didn't hear her—uttered the word, "Again." So Spencer repeated the action at her command. Again. And again. And again.

He dropped to his knees with a rough groan, pressing his mouth to her flat belly, curling his fingers into the waistband of her jeans to hold her in place. He ached to take her right here, right now, quickly, deeply, passionately. But he wouldn't do that tonight. There would be times in the future when their lovemaking could rush at a rabid, terrifying pace. Just not tonight.

"I'll admit it's scary what happens when we're together," he told her, trying to keep his breathing steady. "And I'll concede that sometimes it feels like it goes beyond our control. But I won't hurt you, Roxy," he whispered against her warm flesh. "I would never hurt you. I want to be inside you, the way you're inside me. I love you. I don't want to own you."

He felt her fingers curling tightly in his hair, but he wasn't sure if she was encouraging him or trying to push him away. So he moved his head away from her belly to gaze up at her. And when he did, her fingers fell to the snap at her waist and fumbled to undo it.

"Let me," he said, his hands immediately replacing hers.

With quick, deft fingers, he unfastened the metal snap and tugged down the zipper, spreading the heavy denim open wide to reveal the smooth, flat plane of her belly. Sapphire blue satin dipped low enough for him to see the shadow of dark hair that covered that most intimate part of her, and he couldn't help himself when he pressed his head to her and trailed his tongue along the irregular line.

He felt Roxy sway against him and cupped her fanny with both hands, holding her still until she recovered. Then he clenched the blue jeans in his fists and tugged them down over her hips, dragging her panties along with them. Without balking, she toed off her shoes and stepped out of the garments, then stood before Spencer, flagrantly naked.

He dipped his head to her belly, breathing in the musky scent of her, and she tangled her fingers in his hair once again. For a long moment, he only knelt there before her, almost as if he were offering up a prayer. Then he circled her ankles with his fingers and slowly, so slowly, drew his loosely fisted hands up over her calves and knees, splaying his hands open over her thighs before settling them resolutely on her hips. He pulled her forward then, opening his mouth over her navel, tasting the sweet indentation with his tongue.

Again, she began to lose her footing, so he gripped her buttocks firmly in his hands, his fingers deftly invading the cleft that separated them. And when she swayed forward, he opened his mouth against her, suckling her fully, exploring her deeply. His tongue darted against the sensitive nub that defined her sexuality, then flattened to taste her completely. He heard her groan and felt her fingers tighten in his hair.

"Oh, Spencer," she whispered.

But she said nothing more, and whether she liked what he was doing or felt shamed by it, he didn't know. So he moved away from her and stood, taking her hands in his and placing them on the button placket of his shirt.

"Your turn," he said. "I'm yours. Do with me what you will."

Her fingers tightened on his shirt for a moment, then she glanced over her shoulder, at the front windows. Although the curtains were drawn, he could tell she felt some trepidation in the living room.

"Take me upstairs," she told him.

Immediately, he swept her up in his arms and carried her to the stairway. She unfastened his shirt buttons one by one as they proceeded, shoving the garment from his shoulders. He left it unheeded where it fell on the stairs, and she tugged his T-shirt from the waistband of his trousers.

When they arrived in his room, he set her on her feet and she quickly tugged his shirt up over his head. Then her fingers dropped to the fastening of his trousers, and as capably as he had removed her clothes, she helped him out of the rest of his. But where he had loosely circled her ankles, she curled her fingers over the base of a different part of him, gliding her warm palm up the length of him to graze her thumb gently over its tip.

Spencer sucked in a ragged breath and held it, willing himself not to overreact. But the idle meanderings of her hand made it impossible for him to stay sane. He dropped his own hand to cover hers, curving her fingers more insistently against himself, guiding both of their hands back and forth along his shaft.

Roxy leaned into him, burying her face in the thick, dark hair on his chest, laving his flat nipples with her tongue before nipping them playfully with her teeth. Her other hand dropped to his hip, her fingers pressing into his taut flesh, dipping to the back of his thigh. She rubbed her body against his, then began to take her kisses lower. Slowly, she fell to her knees in the same way he had been only moments ago, and Spencer raked his fingers through her hair.

"Last time," she whispered against him, "you took care of me. This time, I'll take care of you."

Vaguely, he registered the fact that the words she used were the words she'd claimed to abhor a short time ago, and somehow his mind registered that this was a good thing. Then his mind ceased to function at all, because his senses seized control, working overtime to absorb all the things she was doing to him.

Just when he thought his frenetic heartbeat would make the organ explode in his chest, Roxy rose to stand before him, and without losing a moment, Spencer pulled her flush against him, then backed her to the bed in a slow, erratic stroll. He bent her backward over the mattress, one hand cradling the small of her back, the other dipping between her legs to spread her thighs. He fingered her delicately for a moment, and her head fell back wildly, her breasts beckoning to him again. So he bent forward to suckle one, his hand dancing wildly over that heated, heavy heart of her. And when she cried out, he lowered her to the bed and entered her deeply with one massive thrust.

Roxy went absolutely still when she felt him sheathed tightly inside her. Nothing had ever felt more perfect, more right, more complete. What Spencer made her feel was nothing like what she had experienced when she was a green, uncertain adolescent. Yes, she'd lost a part of herself to him, perhaps the moment she'd met him. But he'd offered her part of himself in return, to fill the empty places inside her. That was one thing Reggie had never done. He'd never given her anything.

Spencer had given her everything. All that was in him, he had surrendered to her. And she had absorbed it into every pore, every nerve, every cell. She supposed that was what happened when a person fell in love. She shared. Of herself, of her life, of her love. She gave and received and enjoyed. And suddenly, somehow, Roxy felt stronger than she ever had in her life. She had the strength of two people now—she would never have to fight alone again. And neither would Spencer, she promised herself. Together, they could create magic.

He withdrew from her, and she murmured her objection, then felt him rush deep inside her again. He moved his hand between her legs to tease her again, pumping in and out of her, over and over, until she wasn't sure exactly where he was.

Oh, wait, she thought hazily. Yes, she did. She knew exactly where Spencer was. Where he would always be. She gripped him more fiercely and pulled him against her again, shuddering at the explosion of heat he brought with him. She cried out at the welcoming warmth that spilled into her when he emptied himself inside her, filling her with so much…so many things she had never thought she would feel. Then he fell to the bed beside her, drawing her close, wrapping her in his arms, burying his head in her shoulder.

"I love you," he vowed on a ragged breath. "I love you."

Somehow she managed to lift her hand and cup the back of his head. She turned her body to his, pressing against him, pulling him as close as she could. "I love you, too," she murmured against his cheek, punctuating the vow with a tender kiss. "I love you, too."

For a long time, neither of them spoke or moved. They only lay entwined and exhausted, dazed and dizzy, contemplative and complete. Spencer was the first to move. He rose above Roxy, resting his head in his hand, his elbow propped on the mattress beside her head.

"Did you say what I think you said?" he asked her quietly.

She nodded. "Yes."

"Do you really love me?"

She nodded again, but said nothing.

"Then tell me so. Again."

"I love you."

He smiled, brushing her damp hair away from her forehead, skimming his fingertips over her cheek. "What made you change your mind?"

She narrowed her eyes at him, then lifted her hand to cup his cheek. "I'm not sure I did change my mind," she said. "I think I've loved you since the beginning. I just had to work through some things before I could admit it."

She, too, caressed his face with tentative fingers, then lifted her head to kiss him chastely on the lips. "What happened with Reggie…" she began again, "it's defined my life since then. I've never been able to let myself feel too deeply for anyone. And I've always told myself I'm uncomfortable around wealthy people, because they reminded me of Reggie."

Her eyes darkened some, but they met his gaze levelly. "But for some reason, I've never felt uncomfortable around you. In your house, at your office, at that party tonight. I never felt out of place. And I think that's because you were there with me. You just…" She paused for a moment, then smiled. "You feel right, Spencer. You feel good. You feel…natural."

He chuckled. "Well, I hate to say I told you so, but…"

She chuckled, too, but felt a little melancholy. "You've given me so much, Spencer. You'll never know how much. After Bingo died, I figured I was going to be alone forever, and—"

He touched one finger gently to her mouth. "Don't say it," he told her. "I know exactly what you mean. But, Roxy, neither one of us is ever going to be alone again. With or without my lost twin, I've found a family. Because I've found you."

"We'll find Charlotte," she told him quickly. "I promise you that."

He nodded, but he, too, seemed a bit wistful and sad. "I don't doubt it. But even if we don't—"

"We will."

"I'll be a happy man," he finished. He gathered her close, one arm settled around her shoulder, the other draped over her belly. "I have everything I need right here. With you. You're my family now, Roxy. Let me be yours."

She smiled. "Are you proposing what I think you're proposing?"

"I'm proposing. Period."

"Then I'm accepting."

He laughed, splaying his fingers open over her breast. "What say we get started on the honeymoon a little early?"

"Mmm," she murmured agreeably. "But we can't stay up too late. I have to work tomorrow. I have to find some guy's twin sister."

Spencer nodded and nuzzled her neck. "I've waited this long," he told her. "For so many things. Let's not rush any of them. Let's do them right."

Roxy sighed and sank deeper into bed and told him that was fine with her.

Epilogue

"**S**pencer, hurry up. We're going to be late."

Spencer rolled his eyes as he looked into the bathroom mirror and adjusted his shirt one final time. "And I'm sure you're extremely concerned about that."

"Of course I am," Roxy called from the other side of the open door. "I don't want to listen to Mrs. Edna Bison Morrow Van Meter bitching and moaning about us being late again."

"That's Bighton, not Bison," Spencer corrected her as he stuck his head through the door and glanced at the woman standing in the middle of his—or rather, their—bedroom. "Call her Mrs. Bison again, and she'll never invite us back to her house."

Roxy smiled a little too sweetly, and he realized that that, of course, was her plan.

"Fine," he told her. "We won't accept any more invitations to the annual Van Meter Charity Masquerade. If you want, we can send our regrets tonight, along with a nice, fat check."

"What, and waste two perfectly good costumes?"

Spencer chuckled. As always, they had decided to approach the situation in completely different ways. The annual Van Meter Charity Masquerade was one of the poshest, most respected, most attended soirees in the D.C. area, made famous by celebrities from all fields—politics, entertainment, business, the military. Spencer had opted to go this year as a dashing Captain Kidd, and had spent a small fortune renting a pirate costume created by a local designer.

Roxy, on the other hand, had spent three bucks on a used hockey mask, and had rifled through the kitchen until she'd located a bottle of ketchup and a butcher knife. She was going as Jason from the *Friday the 13th* movies, complete with a torn and bloodied Camp Windsock T-shirt. She would be the talk of the party, Spencer was certain. And the general consensus of that talk would be from people uttering, "I wish I'd thought of that...!"

"No, I guess we don't want to waste two perfectly good costumes," he agreed dryly, wishing *he'd* thought of Jason before Roxy had.

He wasn't particularly comfortable in thigh-high leather boots and a shirt that gaped open nearly to his navel. Even if Roxy *had* seemed to be eyeing him in a whole new light since he put the getup on, with a number of sexually explicit ideas obviously parading through her brain.

"Although," she conceded, giving him the once-over again, "I don't guess they'd have to go to waste if we found some other...use...for them."

He eyed her back. "Oh? Like what?"

She shrugged. "Oh, I don't know. But you do look pretty sexy all dressed up like Bluebeard."

"Captain Kidd," he corrected her. "I have no intention of murdering my wife."

She smiled again. "Well, I suppose that's something, seeing as how you've only had one for a few months."

He strode across the room and pulled her into his arms. "You're something," he corrected her, shoving the hockey mask to the top of her head. "You know, I've never made love to a woman in a hockey mask before. Could be pretty kinky.''

She wiggled her eyebrows playfully. ''I could go downstairs and put the ketchup back. Bring up a canister of whipped cream instead.''

''Now *that* sounds like a very good idea. I like the way you think, Roxy Matheny-Melbourne. I've never made love to a woman covered in whipped cream, either. This really could be a night for firsts.''

She smiled again, and this time there was something decidedly secretive about the gesture. Not bad secretive, just...secretive. She knew something he didn't. And he really, really wanted to find out what that was. However, when she remained silent, he realized he was going to have to try another tactic to get her talking.

''And I like the way you dress,'' he added, running a thumb over the ketchup-stained T-shirt.

She laughed, then looped her arms around his waist, but still she said nothing to reveal what she was thinking.

''And I like the way you *un*dress, too,'' he continued, dropping a hand to the waistband of that T-shirt, splaying his hand open over her warm skin.

Playfully, Roxy brushed his hand back to his side and danced away from him. ''I have a question,'' she announced, laughing at the confusion he knew must be obvious on his face.

''About what? I thought we were both pretty well decided on what we were going to do this evening.''

She shook her head. ''There's something I have to have cleared up first.''

''Okay. Shoot.''

She tented her fingertips together, still smiling, and eyed him thoughtfully. ''You say you've never made love to a woman in a hockey mask before.''

He nodded. ''That's true. I haven't.''

''And that you've never made love to a woman covered with whipped cream before, either.''

He nodded again. "That's going to be a new one for me, too."

"How about…a pregnant woman? Ever made love to one of those?"

Spencer opened his mouth to automatically reply in the negative again before the import of her words struck him. For a moment, he only studied her through narrowed eyes. Then he began to smile, too.

"Are you saying what I think you're saying?"

She nodded. "That you're about to seduce a whipped-cream-covered, mass-murdering mother-to-be."

He laughed. "You know, I heard those pregnancy hormones could be killers, but I never suspected…"

She laughed, too, then sprang back into his arms, kissing him soundly on the mouth.

"You're sure?" he asked when she ended the kiss. "I mean, this isn't just something you suspect?"

She dipped her head to nuzzle his neck and shook her head. "Two home pregnancy tests have come back positive. When I called the doctor's office, they said that pretty much clinches it, but that they'd take another one anyway when I come in for my first prenatal check."

Spencer said nothing for a moment, just let the information seep into his brain. He was going to find out what it was like, he thought. All of it. That whole mysterious, circling bond of husband-wife, parent-child, family union. He was going to have more than he ever thought he would have. By launching the search for his missing twin, he would end up with more than he had ever bargained for. And nothing in the world could make him happier than he was right now.

This was some family plan he'd found for himself.

"That settles it," he finally said, resting his chin atop her head and hugging her close. "We're not going anywhere tonight. We're celebrating. At home. As a family."

He felt Roxy nod her head against his chest. "Home," she repeated softly. "Funny, that's a word I never thought I'd find myself using too often. It's something I never thought I'd have. Not really. Not like this."

Spencer rubbed his cheek against her hair, hugging her more tightly still. "And family," he repeated just as quietly. "That's something I never thought *I'd* have. Not really. Not like this."

He pulled away from her some, enough to gaze down at her face. "I never thought I'd find even one family," he said. "Now, thanks to you, I'm going to have two."

She smiled back up at him. "Maybe. We still haven't found Charlotte."

"But we will," he said with quiet confidence. "We will. And when we do, I know she'll be thrilled to discover she's going to be an auntie."

Roxy laughed. "Who knows? Maybe we'll have twins."

Spencer nodded. "Whatever it is, it's going to be perfect. For all of us. You, me, our baby, my sister. All of us will have a family. And none of us will ever have to be alone again."

And for Spencer, that was all that mattered.

*   *   *   *   *

Watch for the continuing story of
THE FAMILY McCORMICK as we meet Spencer's
twin in Lucy and the Loner, coming in April from
Silhouette Desire.

TRACI ON THE SPOT   BY TRACI

1

Morgan Brigham slowly set down his coffee cup on the kitchen table and stared at the comic strip in the center of his paper. It was nestled in among approximately twenty others that were spread out across two pages. But this was the only one he made a point of reading faithfully each morning at breakfast.

This was the only one that mirrored *her* life.

He read each panel twice, as if he couldn't trust his own eyes. But he could. It was there, in black and white.

Morgan folded the paper slowly, thoughtfully, his mind not on his task. So Traci was getting engaged.

The realization gnawed at the lining of his stomach. He hadn't a clue as to why.

He had even less of a clue why he did what he did next.

Abandoning his coffee, now cool, and the newspaper, and ignoring the fact that this was going to make him late for the office, Morgan went to get a sheet of stationery from the den.

He didn't have much time.

Traci Richardson stared at the last frame she had just drawn. Debating, she glanced at the creature sprawled out on the kitchen floor.

"What do you think, Jeremiah? Too blunt?"

The dog, part bloodhound, part mutt, idly looked up from his rawhide bone at the sound of his name. Jeremiah gave her a look she felt free to interpret as ambivalent.

"Fine help you are. What if Daniel actually reads this and puts two and two together?"

Not that there was all that much chance that the man who had proposed to her, the very prosperous and busy Dr. Daniel Thane, would actually see the comic strip she drew for a living. Not unless the strip was taped to a bicuspid he was examining. Lately Daniel had gotten so busy he'd stopped reading anything but the morning headlines of the *Times*.

Still, you never knew. "I don't want to hurt his feelings," Traci continued, using Jeremiah as a sounding board. "It's just that Traci is overwhelmed by Donald's proposal and, see, she thinks the ring is going to swallow her up." To prove her point, Traci held up the drawing for the dog to view.

This time, he didn't even bother to lift his head.

Traci stared moodily at the small velvet box on the kitchen counter. It had sat there since Daniel had asked her to marry him last Sunday. Even if Daniel never read her comic strip, he was going to suspect something eventually. The very fact that she hadn't grabbed the ring from his hand and slid it onto her finger should have told him that she had doubts about their union.

Traci sighed. Daniel was a catch by any definition. So what was her problem? She kept waiting to be struck by that sunny ray of happiness. Daniel said he wanted to take care of her, to fulfill her every wish. And he was even willing to let her think about it before she gave him her answer.

Guilt nibbled at her. She should be dancing up and down, not wavering like a weather vane in a gale.

Pronouncing the strip completed, she scribbled her signature in the corner of the last frame and then sighed. Another week's work put to bed. She glanced at the pile of mail on the counter. She'd been bringing it in steadily from the mailbox since Monday, but the stack had gotten no farther than her kitchen. Sorting letters seemed the least heinous of all the annoying chores that faced her.

Traci paused as she noted a long envelope. Morgan Brigham. Why would Morgan be writing to her?

Curious, she tore open the envelope and quickly scanned the short note inside.

Dear Traci,
I'm putting the summerhouse up for sale. Thought you might want to come up and see it one more time before it goes up on the block. Or make a bid for it yourself. If memory serves, you once said you wanted to buy it. Either way, let me know. My number's on the card.

Take care,
Morgan

P.S. Got a kick out of *Traci on the Spot* this week.

Traci folded the letter. He read her strip. She hadn't known that. A feeling of pride silently coaxed a smile to her lips. After a beat, though, the rest of his note seeped into her consciousness. He was selling the house.

The summerhouse. A faded white building with brick trim. Suddenly, memories flooded her mind. Long, lazy afternoons that felt as if they would never end.

Morgan.

She looked at the far wall in the family room. There was a large framed photograph of her and Morgan standing before the summerhouse. Traci and Morgan. Morgan and Traci. Back then, it seemed their lives had been permanently intertwined. A bittersweet feeling of loss passed over her.

Traci quickly pulled the telephone over to her on the counter and tapped out the number on the keypad.

* * * * *

*Look for TRACI ON THE SPOT
by Marie Ferrarella, coming to
Silhouette YOURS TRULY
in March 1997.*

MILLION DOLLAR SWEEPSTAKES
OFFICIAL RULES
NO PURCHASE NECESSARY TO ENTER

1. To enter, follow the directions published. Method of entry may vary. For eligibility, entries must be received no later than March 31, 1998. No liability is assumed for printing errors, lost, late, non-delivered or misdirected entries.

   To determine winners, the sweepstakes numbers assigned to submitted entries will be compared against a list of randomly, preselected prize winning numbers. In the event all prizes are not claimed via the return of prize winning numbers, random drawings will be held from among all other entries received to award unclaimed prizes.

2. Prize winners will be determined no later than June 30, 1998. Selection of winning numbers and random drawings are under the supervision of D. L. Blair, Inc., an independent judging organization whose decisions are final. Limit: one prize to a family or organization. No substitution will be made for any prize, except as offered. Taxes and duties on all prizes are the sole responsibility of winners. Winners will be notified by mail. Odds of winning are determined by the number of eligible entries distributed and received.

3. Sweepstakes open to residents of the U.S. (except Puerto Rico), Canada and Europe who are 18 years of age or older, except employees and immediate family members of Torstar Corp., D. L. Blair, Inc., their affiliates, subsidiaries, and all other agencies, entities, and persons connected with the use, marketing or conduct of this sweepstakes. All applicable laws and regulations apply. Sweepstakes offer void wherever prohibited by law. Any litigation within the province of Quebec respecting the conduct and awarding of a prize in this sweepstakes must be submitted to the Régie des alcools, des courses et des jeux. In order to win a prize, residents of Canada will be required to correctly answer a time-limited arithmetical skill-testing question to be administered by mail.

4. Winners of major prizes (Grand through Fourth) will be obligated to sign and return an Affidavit of Eligibility and Release of Liability within 30 days of notification. In the event of non-compliance within this time period or if a prize is returned as undeliverable, D. L. Blair, Inc. may at its sole discretion, award that prize to an alternate winner. By acceptance of their prize, winners consent to use of their names, photographs or other likeness for purposes of advertising, trade and promotion on behalf of Torstar Corp., its affiliates and subsidiaries, without further compensation unless prohibited by law. Torstar Corp. and D. L. Blair, Inc., their affiliates and subsidiaries are not responsible for errors in printing of sweepstakes and prize winning numbers. In the event a duplication of a prize winning number occurs, a random drawing will be held from among all entries received with that prize winning number to award that prize.

5. This sweepstakes is presented by Torstar Corp., its subsidiaries and affiliates in conjunction with book, merchandise and/or product offerings. The number of prizes to be awarded and their value are as follows: Grand Prize — $1,000,000 (payable at $33,333.33 a year for 30 years); First Prize — $50,000; Second Prize — $10,000; Third Prize — $5,000; 3 Fourth Prizes — $1,000 each; 10 Fifth Prizes — $250 each; 1,000 Sixth Prizes — $10 each. Values of all prizes are in U.C. currency. Prizes in each level will be presented in different creative executions, including various currencies, vehicles, merchandise and travel. Any presentation of a prize level in a currency other than U.S. currency represents an approximate equivalent to the U.S. currency prize for that level, at that time. Prize winners will have the opportunity of selecting any prize offered for that level; however, the actual non U.S. currency equivalent prize if offered and selected, shall be awarded at the exchange rate existing at 3:00 P.M. New York time on March 31, 1998. A travel prize option, if offered and selected by winner, must be completed within 12 months of selection and is subject to: traveling companion(s) completing and returning of a Release of Liability prior to travel; and hotel and flight accommodations availability. For a current list of all prize options offered within prize levels, send a self-addressed, stamped envelope (WA residents need not affix postage) to: MILLION DOLLAR SWEEPSTAKES Prize Options, P.O. Box 4456, Blair, NE 68009-4456, USA.

6. For a list of prize winners (available after July 31, 1998) send a separate, stamped, self-addressed envelope to: MILLION DOLLAR SWEEPSTAKES Winners, P.O. Box 4459, Blair, NE 68009-4459, USA.

SWP-FEB97

As seen on TV!
Free Gift Offer

With a Free Gift proof-of-purchase from any Silhouette® book, you can receive a beautiful cubic zirconia pendant.

This gorgeous marquise-shaped stone is a genuine cubic zirconia—accented by an 18" gold tone necklace.

(Approximate retail value $19.95)

Send for yours today...
compliments of ▼ *Silhouette*®
™

To receive your free gift, a cubic zirconia pendant, send us one original proof-of-purchase, photocopies not accepted, from the back of any Silhouette Romance™, Silhouette Desire®, Silhouette Special Edition®, Silhouette Intimate Moments® or Silhouette Yours Truly™ title available in February, March and April at your favorite retail outlet, together with the Free Gift Certificate, plus a check or money order for $1.65 u.s./$2.15 can. (do not send cash) to cover postage and handling, payable to Silhouette Free Gift Offer. We will send you the specified gift. Allow 6 to 8 weeks for delivery. Offer good until April 30, 1997 or while quantities last. Offer valid in the U.S. and Canada only.

Free Gift Certificate

Name: _____

Address: _____

City: _____ State/Province: _____ Zip/Postal Code: _____

Mail this certificate, one proof-of-purchase and a check or money order for postage and handling to: SILHOUETTE FREE GIFT OFFER 1997. In the U.S.: 3010 Walden Avenue, P.O. Box 9077, Buffalo NY 14269-9077. In Canada: P.O. Box 613, Fort Erie, Ontario L2Z 5X3.

FREE GIFT OFFER   084-KFD
ONE PROOF-OF-PURCHASE
To collect your fabulous FREE GIFT, a cubic zirconia pendant, you must include this original proof-of-purchase for each gift with the properly completed Free Gift Certificate.

In February, Silhouette Books is proud
to present the sweeping, sensual new novel
by bestselling author

CAIT LONDON

about her unforgettable family—*The Tallchiefs.*

Everyone in Amen Flats, Wyoming, was talking about
Elspeth Tallchief. How she wasn't a thirty-three-year-old
virgin, after all. How she'd been keeping herself warm at
night all these years with a couple of secrets. And now one
of those secrets had walked right into town, sending
everyone into a frenzy. But Elspeth knew he'd come for
the *other* secret....

"Cait London is an irresistible storyteller..."

—*Romantic Times*

Don't miss TALLCHIEF FOR KEEPS by Cait London, available
at your favorite retail outlet in February from

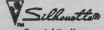

CLST

SILHOUETTE® *Desire®*

COMING NEXT MONTH

#1057 TIGHT-FITTIN' JEANS—Mary Lynn Baxter

Garth Dixon, March's *Man of the Month*, had given up on love and marriage, but the way city girl Tiffany Russell looked in her jeans took his breath away. If Garth wasn't careful, he'd find himself escorting her down the aisle!

#1058 THE FIVE-MINUTE BRIDE—Leanne Banks

How To Catch a Princess

Emily St. Clair always dreamed of marrying her own Prince Charming, so she ran away from her wedding into the arms of rough and rugged sheriff Beau Ramsey. If only Beau wasn't so set on his bachelor ways!

#1059 HAVE BRIDE, NEED GROOM—Maureen Child

Jenny Blake needed a husband—fast! She had only four days to get married and stop the family curse. So she risked everything and married reluctant groom Nick Tarantelli for one year's time....

#1060 A BABY FOR MOMMY—Sara Orwig

Micah Drake wasn't certain if the beautiful amnesiac woman he rescued was single and available...or her married twin sister. But one thing was clear—making love to this woman was a risk he was willing to take.

#1061 WEDDING FEVER—Susan Crosby

Maggie Walters's wish to be a bride by her thirtieth birthday finally came true—unfortunately, groom J.D. Duran was marrying her only to protect her. But J.D. soon discovered *he* was the one in danger...of losing his heart.

#1062 PRACTICE HUSBAND—Judith McWilliams

Joe Barrington was not a marrying man. But when Joe found himself teaching his friend Addy Edson how to attract a husband, would Addy's enticing ways lure him into marriage?

Harlequin and Silhouette celebrate
Black History Month with seven terrific titles,
featuring the all-new *Fever Rising*
by Maggie Ferguson
(Harlequin Intrigue #408) and
A Family Wedding by Angela Benson
(Silhouette Special Edition #1085)!

Also available are:
Looks Are Deceiving by Maggie Ferguson
Crime of Passion by Maggie Ferguson
Adam and Eva by Sandra Kitt
Unforgivable by Joyce McGill
Blood Sympathy by Reginald Hill

On sale in January at your favorite
Harlequin and Silhouette retail outlet.

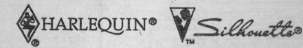

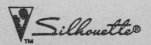